THE KITCHEN FABLE

On the Mythical Origins of the World's Most Useful Sandwich

TIM KNUTSON

This is a work of fiction. The names, characters, and incidents are the product of the author's imagination. Any resemblance to actual people, living or dead, events, or locales is entirely coincidental.

Cover illustration by Lauren Marvell – laurenmarvell.com

In loving memory of two kitchen masters
Peter Mahler and Diane Knutson

Miss Betty's Diner—2005

"Mom, I'm sorry about the broken dishes tonight. Miss Jenny said you were really mad."

"I was, Joshua, but that was just in the moment."

It was the third time in the last two months that Joshua had some friends over. He seemed to be growing quite popular with his classmates. She was certain he had more friends than she did.

She let out a sigh of relief. Money was tight for the owner of Miss Betty's Diner. Thankfully her kid and his friends thought that having a pop dispenser at their disposal was living in luxury.

"Joshua, you know that it costs money to replace things like broken dishes, right?"

"Yeah, I know."

"Well, we don't have a lot of money right now. That's why I was upset at first. However, I'm really glad that you're making friends at school. Penelope and Brady seem like nice kids."

"They are. And they're sorry too."

"I know you are. And I know they are, but I want to tell you something else. There are a lot of things in life that you can buy, like a house, a car, clothes, dishes, and other stuff."

She continued, "One thing you can't buy is community. You have to build that. So, even though I was mad for a moment about the broken dishes, I'm happy to see you making friends and building your community. Now you better get upstairs to bed. It's late."

Part One—2025

1—On the Origins of a Beloved Sandwich

What if peanut butter and jelly sandwiches never existed? How would the world react upon tasting one for the first time? Shall we find out?

"Mom Betty, what was that sandwich you made me last week?"

"You mean the jelly and peanut butter on my cottage bread?"

"Yeah, that's the one. Can I have another one of those today?"

"I can make you anything on the menu, Brady."

"No thank you. I've been craving one all week."

"You know, I started making these for Joshua when he was such a picky eater as a kid. I never put it on the menu on account of it being so simple. Anyone can make one at home."

"I suppose so, but if that's true, why haven't I ever heard of it before?"

"Here you go. One grape jelly and peanut butter sandwich."

Betty Einfach opened the eponymous Miss Betty's Diner back in 1994, having ventured to the town of El Grain, Wisconsin, for a job that didn't last but four weeks. During that time, she made just enough money that she could afford the first and last month's rent at the former Connie's Café. Just off the main drag, the diner had a one-bedroom upstairs apartment that came with the rent. Now, thirty years later, at fifty-eight years old, she owned the building outright. The owner put the building up for sale in 2008 to satisfy some other debts. Betty hated the thought of losing her diner to the whims of a new owner so she bought the building. Since then, she'd converted the apartment to additional seating and bought some acreage outside of town to build a cozy A-frame in a pine-oak forest.

Her only child, Joshua, was born in 1995, just a year after her arrival in El Grain. She knew who the father was, but he denied it, claiming that it must've been another guy, or even a virgin birth—you know, like Jesus. She didn't push the issue; who wants to raise a kid with a father who has no interest in his son? She dated a bit when Joshua was in grade school, but she always felt judged by the community as a newcomer and how it was that she came to live in El Grain. So, nothing ever got too serious. She stopped trying to meet someone right around the time Joshua decided that his name was Josh.

"You know, for as much as Josh and I hung out at your place growing up, I'm surprised I never had one of these sandwiches before last week."

"That doesn't shock me, Brady. I would never have given you something so basic back then. When you were growing up, I always felt the town's eyes on me so I made sure to put my best effort into every meal. Thankfully I was a good cook and people's hunger outweighed their judgment. Otherwise this diner never would've made it. I figure two years from now, I'll even be considered a local."

Brady Samuels smiled wryly at the woman he knew as Mom Betty. Brady and Josh were inseparable as kids, two-thirds of the Rogue Collective, as they called themselves. They ventured apart after high school. Josh went to college in Madison while Brady stayed closer to home, taking a job at the frac sand mining operation on the outskirts of town. Smartphones kept them connected even as Josh moved further east after college and law school. He was currently on a partner track at a mid-sized law office in Milwaukee. Penelope Barnes was the third rogue among them. She took advantage of tuition reciprocity and studied marketing at the University of Minnesota, ultimately accepting a job in St. Paul. Recognizing the distance between them, Brady's birthday request was a weekend campout with some old high school friends.

"So, does this one feel any different?"

"No. It's just as good as the last one. It might even be better."

"I meant your birthday. You're completing your thirtieth lap, right?"

"No. Just starting number thirty. I've only got Josh by a few months."

"That's what I meant. Our age is always the number of years we've completed."

"I don't think so. I'm turning thirty, so I'll be thirty for this whole coming year."

"It is kind of a silly thing to disagree on, isn't it? Let me say it this way. When does a baby turn one?"

"When they've lived one year."

"Do you see it now?"

It took him a moment, but she let his mind work so that he could own the realization. Once it clicked he wasn't angry but excited over a simple fact that he'd never taken the time to contemplate. Betty Einfach had a gentle way about her. She wasn't afraid to disagree with someone, but she was good at finding a way of doing so without injuring her neighbor's ego. Sometime over the years she had been trained to explain people's quirks and behaviors in the kindest way. Being gracious had served her well. After all, who was she to judge?

"Mom Betty, did you ever think about teaching when you were younger?"

"I do like the idea of summer break, but that's hard to do without a college degree. I had Joshua. The diner. College didn't fit."

"You would've been a good teacher. I mean, you are. Even if your classroom is a diner. Welp, I suppose I should get my stuff together before we head out."

"OK, but do me a favor if you see Joshua before I do. Tell him I made about a dozen sandwiches for your campout on the sand bar tonight. They travel well, but he's got to come say hi to his mother to get them."

"Jelly and peanut butter?"

"You betcha."

"I thought you didn't serve those to Josh's friends. Too many judgy people, or something like that?"

"That was when I was a young mother. I'm older now. I don't have the energy to care what other people think of me. Besides, it's a good sandwich."

2—On Eating Sandwiches on a Sand Bar

Sandwiched between Lansing, Iowa, and DeSoto, Wisconsin, are dozens of islands, bays, nooks, and crannies on either side of the main channel of the Mississippi River. Camping on a sand bar watching the barges go by, it's easy to feel removed from modern society. It was also a great place to build a campfire, drink some beers, and hang out with old high school friends on your thirtieth birthday.

Brady and Joshua left for the sand bar shortly after Josh got to town, said hi to his mom, and grabbed the food she had prepared. Four of the six friends still lived near El Grain. Only Josh and Penny moved out of town. Matt also left town for college, but he came back to teach history at both the high school and middle school. Brady had ten years in at Silica Solutions frac sand mining. Tom worked at his dad's hardware store and Ana was a budding real estate agent after several years as a secretary at the insurance company in town. Tom and Ana were married to each other. Matt married Jess, whom he met at college. She would normally tag along, but with a newborn at home she used that excuse to avoid peeing in a portable toilet.

Brady looked forward to the change of pace. He had a regular group of guys that he went drinking with on weekday nights, but he wanted to see his old friends for this momentous birthday.

For Betty, the few minutes of seeing Joshua before his campout was hardly enough, but she knew he'd be back on Sunday afternoon and didn't have to head back to Milwaukee until Monday night.

That plan was intentional, given that Miss Betty's Diner was closed on Mondays. It did make her a little sad that she didn't get to see the rest of the gang before they headed out. She recalled them during childhood playing loudly in the apartment while she was busy downstairs. Occasionally their play spilled out into the diner before Betty or one of the servers shepherded them back up to the apartment. She had always liked Penelope, who had shortened her name around the same time as Joshua.

"So, your mom still want you to get together with Penny?"

"She's laid off of that for a while now. I think she realizes that Minneapolis and Milwaukee are three hundred miles apart."

"I'm sure she's hoping this weekend'll convince you otherwise, or at least get you thinking about moving back this way."

"I don't know. She's talked about moving out of El Grain when she retires. Maybe even moving back to the Twin Cities. My aunt lives in Bloomington. They're pretty close."

"Of course. Don't you see it? Penny's already in the Cities. Mom Betty will move there in retirement. They'll work on getting you to move up there. Then she'll get you two married off and she'll be living nearby to take care of the grandkids. Your mom's no dummy. She's way smarter than me."

"That could be her thinking, but Penny and I have never clicked like that. I don't know what it's like to have a sister, but I kind of imagine it's like what Penny and I have."

"If you say so. And, if that's the case, mind if I ask your sister for a date?"

As they approached the boat landing, the conversation shifted and the question was left dangling. Neither seemed too concerned, but they'd just come dangerously close to having a real conversation about emotions and relationships.

They unloaded the canoe from the top of the car and set it in the water. Once it was floating, they added their backpacks, a couple of lifejackets, and Lou's Loo—their trusty portable toilet. They still had enough daylight to get out to the sand bar, and thankfully they only had to worry about themselves. The four others planned to travel together on Matt's flat-bottomed johnboat. It wasn't much to look at, but it was perfect for the Mississippi backwaters. Spotting their cars in the parking lot, it looked like the four of them had already made their way over to their preferred sand bar. Judging by the three other cars, it looked like they might not have the island to themselves.

As they approached the spit of land between Iowa and Wisconsin, it became clear that there was in fact another group with a similar plan for the weekend. That was often the case on fall weekends; they could only hope that the other visitors were not a fraternity from the local college or a group of high school teenagers. They bottomed out the canoe on the sandy beach and were relieved to see that it was just a group of four around their age. Out of respect, the groups set up camp about 100 yards from one another so that each could enjoy their well-earned respite from modernity.

As they pulled the canoe to shore, Penny ran over to greet them. Instinctively, both Josh and Brady dropped their gear and spread their arms wide open in preparation for a giant hug. She blew past the both of them, opting to wrap her arms around the portable toilet.

"Where have you guys been? I was just about to break the seal on a river birch, but I'd much rather christen Loo. Better to sit than cop a squat if I don't have to."

"So ladylike, Penny. Glad that city life hasn't refined you too much."

"You can give me a hard time later. Right now I'm gonna find a quiet spot in the woods for this toilet. Got any TP?"

"Yeah, it's in the blue ziplock."

"Great. I'll give you hugs when I'm done."

"Grab some sanitizer first. I want a clean hug."

As she ran off, Josh turned to Brady. "Well, at least that's one less thing we have to haul over to camp."

"If that was you two flirting, I've got nothing to worry about. And, she's not afraid to piss in the woods."

"What's not to like? You're really pushing this, aren't you? Do you really think she'd be interested in dating either of us?"

"I'm just messing with you, but we are turning thirty. Maybe one of us should find a girl to get serious about."

With that they trekked over to the campfire, joining Tom, Ana, and Matt. They were rigging up a fire grate for some brats. It was quite an affair when Matt got involved. His method required the brats to be parboiled in beer, onions, and mustard, before finishing them over an open flame. While the brats were finishing, Matt poured off half of the beer from the frying pan. Wasting half a beer was the most controversial part of his recipe. To the remaining beer and onions he added several tablespoons of butter and a teaspoon of sugar and got the onions to caramelizing. Now, since the brats didn't need much time over the open flame he needed to speed up the browning of the onions. This was why he dumped some of the beer and added a bit of sugar. This was his cheat method for cutting down the time needed to finish the onions in time so they could be used as a topping for the brats. Of course, online recipes will call for an hour to caramelize onions, but those onions are made in a kitchen. Real-life outdoor cooking requires innovation and Matt was just the man for the job.

Joshua had grown accustomed to Usinger, Klement's, and Bunzel's sausages during his time in Milwaukee, but he knew that the brats he'd be having tonight came from Hurt's Locker. The local butcher shop was a third-generation shop, locally famous for their unique brat blends which included a blueberry wild rice brat and a Bloody Mary brat. For a brief moment in 2008 they became regionally famous with the introduction of the Bigelow Brat, an obvious attempt to capitalize on the famous movie name. One cease-and-desist letter from a California lawyer was all it took for Emil Hurt to abandon the use of the movie director's name. He framed the letter and hung it near the register as a point of pride. It was the second most controversial event to ever occur at Hurt's Locker. The first being an article that Emil wrote attacking the need to parboil brats before grilling. Oh, to be so lucky as to have your hot take on brat preparation be the most dramatic event in your life.

Ignoring Emil's advice, Matt was preparing a dozen traditional brats for their beer bath.

"Matt, everything smells great."

"Josh, Brady, glad you made it before nightfall. We're just about ready to eat."

"What do you want me to do with this food I brought? We've got beer and a bunch of sandwiches that my mom made."

"Cooler's outside the tent. The food pack is lying on the ground under that big branch over there."

Matt was always prepared. Further north he'd hang the food pack out of precaution for bears, but this far south it was more about protecting the food from smaller critters. No one wanted to wake up to the sounds of raccoons rummaging through their pancake mix. Even with the benefit of being on an island, it was Matt's nature to protect his food.

"What kind of sandwiches did your mom send? Do they need to be kept cold?"

"No. It's her jelly and peanut butter sandwiches. They'll be fine until lunch tomorrow."

"I can't say I've ever had a jelly and peanut butter sandwich. Are they any good?"

Brady jumped in. "They're from Mom Betty, what do you think?"

"Great. Let's have them for lunch tomorrow. Enough for everyone?"

"Yeah. She sent a dozen or so."

+ + + + +

After the brats were eaten, beer consumed, and a few rounds of six-handed euchre played, the group of old friends turned their attention to the campfire. They embellished old high school stories, downplayed their current successes, and talked late into the evening. After a while they noticed that their neighbors must've headed into their tents as there was no more light coming from their campfire. That was the cue they needed that it was time to get some sleep. The promise of tomorrow was more relaxation—among old friends.

A bit after three in the morning they heard the first of several screams. Ana was the first to awake. She elbowed Tom and they both scampered toward the source of the screaming. They guessed it was their neighbors across the island. Upon arriving, they found three of the four campers were awake and digging through their food packs.

"I can't tell what it got into. There's just not enough light."

"Hi, guys. We're Tom and Ana, heard some commotion and thought we'd ask if we can help."

"Be careful. There was a bear in our camp. He could still be hanging around."

"Really? This far south?"

Ana looked at Tom. "I suppose it's possible." Then she looked at the others. "Are you sure it was a bear?"

"Yes, it got into our food."

"Can you show us?"

With that, a man by the name of Derek showed them the food pack lying on the ground with nuts and berries strewn about. About six feet from the campfire, the food pack looked closed but not particularly protected from animal intrusions.

"Are you sure it wasn't something smaller?"

"No, it wasn't smaller. I heard the noises. It sounded huge." His partner, Claire, felt the need to spread her arms wide to show just how big the beast must've been. Ana looked at Tom and pointed to the tracks in the sand. Tom acknowledged her and spoke up.

"Yeah, it's the middle of the night. With the darkness and water all around us things can sound louder than they actually are. However, take a look at these prints. I think we're looking at opossums."

Before Derek could protest too much, Ana chimed in. "I understand that it's hard to imagine an opossum making so much noise, but a bear sighting this far south—and out on an island—would be pretty remarkable. Do you have any place to store your food that's a bit more secure?"

After a bit more small talk, Ana queried Tom as they headed back to their tent. "Is it opossums or possums?"

"Opossums in America. Possums in Australia."

"You're bullshitting. You have no idea."

"Care to make it interesting?"

"We'll look it up when we get home. Loser does the dishes for a month?"

"You're on. I could use a month off of dish duty."

+ + + + +

Upon finishing breakfast later that morning, they couldn't help but notice that the guests down the way were taking down their tent. Not long after, they made their way over to the sextet of high school friends.

"Say, we just wanted to thank you for helping out last night. Turns out it was raccoons who got into our food. We went back to the tent and heard something return about an hour later. This time we spotted them with our flashlight. They dug into almost everything. They may come your way next."

"Well, at least we know now. Thanks for the update. Matt always hangs our food when we camp. It's an old wilderness habit."

"Since our food is a mess and half eaten, we're going to cut our trip short and head back to civilization."

"Hold on a minute. Say, Josh—do we have enough extra sandwiches from your mom to share with our guests before they head out?"

"Sure. I don't mind. Let me grab some."

That act of kindness was all it took. Derek, Claire, Simon, and Bart fell in love with the sandwiches. They couldn't believe they had never tasted such a great combination. They raved about it so much that Brady told them they should check out Miss Betty's Diner in El Grain if they wanted to meet the creator. Having given up on another night on the island, the foursome decided their weekend adventure may yet be salvageable. Maybe it was kismet, as the four friends had all met as undergrads at Eisleben College in El Grain some ten years ago now.

Now, we certainly don't want to impede the flow of this story to follow every side quest for fun facts that pull us away from our main storyline, but it should be noted that Tom won his bet with Ana. Scientifically speaking, opossums are the marsupials that live in North America while possums are a different, albeit similar animal from Australia. It should also be noted that Ana is protesting Tom's victory, citing the common use of the word possum across the central United States. It does leave one wondering what truth is in our post-modern world, for certainly the Algonquin people seemed unconcerned with European classification systems when they named the opossum—roughly translated as white, small animal.

3—On the Holy Site of Miss Betty's Diner

The four Eisleben College alumni arrived at Miss Betty's Diner in time for the supper hour. Their order consisted of two chicken pot pies, a pot roast, and a humble request for a jelly and peanut butter sandwich. Their server, Jenny Brown, informed them that no such item was on the menu.

"Jenny. Earlier today we were on an island of the Mississippi River. Our food was decimated by some rabid raccoons. A young man, Joshua Einfach, blessed us with some jelly and peanut butter sandwiches. His friend Brady told us that they were the creation of Miss Betty's Diner in El Grain. We are but pilgrims searching for the origin of the world's finest sandwich. My question for you, dear server, does Miss Betty exist? And, if so, is she the creator of this life-altering sandwich?"

"Let me see if she's around," Jenny offered, trying to get out of the awkward conversation. She quickly excused herself.

"Laying it on a little thick there, aren't you, Simon?"

"Food is my business, and I want some answers. This sandwich is going to be huge!"

While waiting, the four pilgrims passed the time retelling their version of the raccoon attack. The collective retelling of the story rendered the elements as true, whether they happened or not. Years from now their friends would know of the dual assault on their sand bar campsite. The first wave, led by a reclusive black bear that rummaged through all of their food before they scared him off. They could only imagine that the bear was this far south desperately searching for late-season food. It was also possible that the bear was beyond his normal range due to some virus or dementia—in that case the bear was probably rabid. It was a good thing the friends escaped such an unpredictable wild creature. The second wave, a family of hostile raccoons, no doubt drawn by the smells of open food that the bear exposed, took the opportunity to enjoy a free meal before they too were chased away by the human inhabitants. Bart was certain that one of the raccoons looked him in the eye, strolled onto a fleece pullover that was lying on the ground, and evacuated his bowels—never breaking eye contact. It was an act of defiance he had never seen from wildlife, except for his childhood cat who used to vomit hairballs into his shoes nearly every night. Thankfully they were interrupted before the tale grew too expansive.

"Excuse me, I'm Betty Einfach. I'm told that one of you is looking for a sandwich of jelly and peanut butter."

"Yes, ma'am. I am Simon Rockwell. We were introduced to your sandwiches on a recent camping trip. I don't see it on the menu, but I'm hoping I might convince you to go off menu for my dinner tonight."

"It's not really a dinner sandwich. It's more of a quick lunch, which is also why it's not on the menu. I'm happy to make you one, but I'll have to charge you the same as other sandwiches. I think the BLT is probably the cheapest. I'll have Jenny ring it up like that. Sound good?"

Simon agreed, sharing that he worked as a freelance food writer from Minneapolis and how he'd love to come back and interview the soon to be famous Miss Betty. Derek, the accountant of the group, reminded him that if he wrote about this experience, he may be able to deduct the cost of their experience as business expenses. Betty had no interest in the tax avoidance strategies of young urban professionals, so she mentioned that Jenny would serve the sandwich with the rest of the meal shortly.

As Jenny arrived with the flaky, golden chicken pot pies and the savory pot roast, the simplicity of the jelly and peanut butter on honey wheat bread was obvious. Betty added sides of coleslaw and grapes so the plate wouldn't look quite so empty. The more they ate, the more convinced they became that the first camp incursion was a bear. It had to be. Raccoons couldn't make that much noise. And, as the food settled in their stomachs, so the cement of their story settled in their minds. They were lucky to have escaped. It could have been much worse. They couldn't understand how those other campers were unfazed. As a matter of fact, maybe that's why the food tasted so good tonight. It was the food of those who barely escaped a perilous situation. They were convinced of it.

Except Simon. While he agreed that they escaped, he was also certain that jelly and peanut butter would taste as good regardless of any added adrenaline. He couldn't stop talking about how this time, the sandwich was on honey wheat, not cottage bread, and it still tasted great. Also, Betty had traded out the grape jelly for strawberry jam. It was simply the work of a food master. He wondered aloud at what other tricks Betty may have up her sleeve. So convinced was he, that he ran to the car and grabbed his notebook in order to ask Miss Betty a few more questions before they left. He also used his mobile phone to snap some exterior photos. He did not want to miss this story. It had to be shared. In this instance, the cutting edge of food exploration did not belong to New York, New Orleans, Portland, or even Austin. No, the best new sandwich of a generation was imagined and created in the heart of Wisconsin, and he was going to break the story.

"Miss Betty?"

"Betty is fine."

"Betty, when I publish this story people are going to want to visit your café. They are going to ask for a jelly and peanut butter sandwich. You'll need to put it on the menu. It's too good to hide."

"Listen. This is just staple food for hungry people. It's three ingredients that nearly any American kitchen has on hand. People aren't going to drive out of their way for this sandwich. If anything, they're going to look in their pantry and realize *I'm hungry* and throw a quick sandwich together."

"So humble. You're the master and you don't even know it. I'll be in touch."

Later, as they were closing up, Jenny and Betty shared a good laugh.

"I didn't know I was working at the feet of a master."

"Oh, hush now. It's not the first time I was told this town was going to make me a big star. Hasn't happened yet, and I hardly think a new sandwich is going to make it so."

"Someone else told you El Grain was going to make you a star?"

"Something like that. It's a story for another day. Why don't you get out of here? I don't want your skin getting burned by my radiance."

4—On Adding a Sandwich to the Menu

"Miss Betty, we've got two more orders for jelly and peanut butter sandwiches. Do we have enough bread to keep up? What should I tell the guests?"

"Don't worry, Hazel, I sent Emilio down to the bakery. We just don't have the time to bake all of our bread in-house anymore. It's a good problem to have."

Hazel was the sixteen-year-old hostess who filled in as an extra server whenever Betty would let her. She loved it, and Betty appreciated her gumption. Enthusiastic workers are often rewarded—especially in hospitality work. And even though Hazel skewed naïve, that innocence reminded many of the early-bird dinner guests of their own granddaughters, and they tipped accordingly.

Miss Betty's Diner was enjoying a fantastic run on the new sandwich. Ever since Betty put the sandwich on the menu, early adopters had been raving about it to anyone who would listen. She didn't necessarily believe the young man Simon, and his promise to write a story, but she did consider his input about adding the new sandwich to her menu.

First, she tried to figure out what sides to add to the plate to make it look like a meal. She tried every soup in her rotation but couldn't find a good partner for a soup and sandwich deal. Tomato—nope. Chili—definitely not. Navy bean—don't even think about it. Butternut squash—better not. Even the versatile chicken noodle soup didn't make for a good pairing. She had to look elsewhere. Ants on a log was OK, if a bit juvenile. The peanut butter on celery sticks with raisins reminded her of packing Joshua's lunch as a kid. Chips worked better than fries, but it still didn't hit the mark. Finally she had Hazel bring in her younger siblings, Harry, Helen, and Henry, to settle things.

They went through nacho chips, pretzel sticks, string cheese, grapes, mandarin oranges in juice, peaches, and a bunch of other options. Eventually Hazel talked to her siblings and they found consensus. Regardless of the jelly flavor, a jelly and peanut butter sandwich should be served with mini pretzels, carrot slices, applesauce, and a homemade cookie. And while Betty didn't trust the naming convention of their parents, she chose to trust the taste buds of the Hartley kids.

Once she knew how she was going to plate the meal, she began to post it as a special for a couple of days each week. She was utterly surprised. That guy Simon was right. Of course there were plenty of regulars who stuck with their favorites, but more and more people were ordering the simple sandwich of jelly and peanut butter. Her freezer full of homemade jams was soon depleted. She had gone through all of her strawberry, grape, peach, blueberry, mixed berry, and strawberry rhubarb. It hadn't mattered what she offered. Every time she pulled a new flavor out of the freezer it was gone within the day. Of course, all of those jams were from her personal supply, but she had never expected the sandwich to take off so she hadn't truly priced jam into her costs.

Having already solved her bread problem, Betty had to find a similar solution for preserves. She reached out to an acquaintance in Hudson who ran a jam business out of her home kitchen and set up an arrangement to become her first commercial customer. It wasn't cheap, so she adjusted the price of the meal. No one was bothered by the new price, they just wanted more jelly and peanut butter sandwiches. She could now offer blackberry, raspberry, currant, and orange marmalade to her list of jelly options. Things were good at Miss Betty's Diner, she just needed to find some more help. Everyone on her team was pretty well maxed out on the help they could provide.

THE KITCHEN FABLE

Arriving early for her shift, Jenny noticed the need for extra help. "Betty, I don't suppose we should look a gift horse in the mouth, because I'm taking home more than ever since you introduced this new sandwich. But this is crazy. What's going to happen if that guy actually writes a story about the diner?"

"You're right, but you might have good cause to wonder why on earth in this day and age someone is giving you a horse as a gift."

5—On Influencers

"Good morning, Minnesota. I'm Jenna Lang."

"And I'm Jana Lang. Welcome to Twin Cities Twins, live from St. Paul."

"Jana, I am so excited to have our first guest back on the show. Simon Rockwell is food editor for *Minnesota Foodie* magazine and popular blogger at *Simon Says Eat Good Food.* You may remember his recent videos from the Minnesota State Fair. He is a food star in the making here in our North Star state."

"I completely agree; but Jenna, he's not here today to talk about Minnesota. He's here to talk about a recent food discovery he made over in El Grain, Wisconsin. He's calling it a generational sandwich. And, not only will he tell us how he discovered this sandwich, but we'll also head over to our test kitchen and make one for ourselves."

"But first, let's check in with Kent Evenson at the news desk. Kent, take it away."

Four years ago, twin sisters Holly and Laura Lang were modestly talented gymnasts for the University of Minnesota. When Covid hit, their gym closed and they could no longer post their cute little videos online. Gymnastics was never their goal. Celebrity was. With life at a standstill, they used April and May of 2020 to rebrand themselves as Jenna and Jana Lang. Being from the Twin Cities, Apple Valley specifically, they wanted to lean into the idea of being twins. They toyed with what names sounded most like twins. Having settled on Jess and Jenna Lang, they were about to change all their social media handles until their dad told them that Jessica

Lange was an Academy Award–winning actress who lived only forty-five minutes away. The discussion got animated, but in the end they decided that Jenna and Jana worked just as well as Jess and Jenna. To this day, it is the only documented instance of a Gen-X father helping his daughters with their social media presence.

Having settled on their new "stage names," Jenna and Jana decided on their hook. Gymnastics was in the past. They would use the summer of 2020 to share their transition from gymnastics to diving. From day one, they would showcase their progress while searching for outdoor places where they could dive during the pandemic lockdown. The first several videos received modest attention. They were at an outdoor pool and each would take turns diving. There wasn't anything particularly unique. Needing to play up the twins angle, they found a pool in Forest Lake that had side by side diving boards. Now they could film their progress by doing synchronous dives. Their videos were garnering more views and they knew they were onto something. Their online presence far exceeded anything they posted as gymnasts, but the challenge was trying to figure out what was next. There were very few pools that were open, and videos from the same pool over and over again wouldn't keep people interested—even if their diving was becoming better.

As June and July came around, it became clear that they needed to move north for the summer to find some good natural diving locations. With the family minivan, a bunch of camera equipment, and a kid brother to document it all, the Langs headed up north. The north shore of Lake Superior provided some stunning opportunities if you could avoid the crowds of everyone who wanted to be outside for the first time in months. To get around this problem, they got up at first light and got to their location by sunrise. The first video that took off was a joint cliff jump near Beaver Bay. Their instincts had proven right. The rock outcroppings of northeastern Minnesota provided plenty of places to jump and dive. It was adventurous enough, and they were photogenic enough to catch people's attention—even if their diving wasn't of the highest quality. They mitigated this criticism by being honest that they were documenting their progress as divers who were once gymnasts. As their skills grew, so did their following.

The following winter, they were hired by a local TV affiliate to produce a segment on the adventures of jumping into a hole in the ice. They parlayed the success of that into a series of online videos for the station, and when the opportunity arose they pitched an hour-long morning show called *Twin Cities Twins*. They didn't know how long their local fame would last, but they were twenty-five-year-olds enjoying the ride. Their segment on jelly and peanut butter sandwiches was about to go viral.

"Simon, welcome back. I think the last time we saw you, you were looking for the best food on a stick at the Great Minnesota Get Together."

"That's right. I'm always looking for new food and I can't wait to tell you about my latest discovery."

"Of course. But first, we have to address the controversy you caused at the state fair. I hate to do this, but we're journalists now. We're totally on your side, so let's clear the air on this."

Being on television does not make one a journalist any more than wearing a robe makes one a judge, but somehow their complete lack of impartiality loosened Simon up and he shared more than he normally would, or should, have.

In his hunt for the best food at the state fair, Simon had a run-in with a chef from a local French-Polynesian fusion restaurant. The chef was upset by Simon's assessment of his food and confronted him while he was filming. Recognizing the situation for what it was, his producer cut the video, but plenty of other state fair attendees whipped out their mobile phones and caught the key part of the exchange.

"So, this is my fault, I let him get under my skin. You can make most of this out on the video, but I told him, 'Foie gras on a stick has to be one of the stupidest ideas for a state fair food I've ever heard of. The whole idea of food at the fair is to make it accessible, there's nothing pretentious about eating deep fried mac and cheese on a stick. You missed the whole point. Maybe you'd realize this if you didn't have a stick so far up your…'"

"Hold up, Simon. Family show here. Family show."

With that they all shared a chuckle and the Lang twins shared a story about their own controversy from October of 2020. Wanting to film a couple more diving videos before winter, the young women and their brother rented a boat to get to their final destination. It wasn't a problem until they took the boat into a restricted wilderness area where no motorized boats were allowed. However, even then it didn't immediately become a problem as it was late in the season and very few people were around. It became a problem when the video got posted and it clearly showed them with a motorized boat at an easily identifiable location. The comment section on their video blew up. People were appalled at the entitled behavior of the twins, and yet their overall number of followers continued to grow.

At first, they denied that they were in a restricted wilderness area. When that didn't work, they claimed that they must've gotten lost amidst the islands on the lake. Finally, they came out with an overly apologetic video acknowledging that they had broken the trust of their viewers and they were sorry for any harm they caused. With this apology, they also made it widely known that to atone for their behavior they were making a donation to the Loons Forever conservation program. One thing missing from the video was any admission that their boat was actually in a restricted area of the Boundary Waters Canoe Area Wilderness. This was on the advice of counsel, for they still faced an inquiry from the US Forest Service regarding their actions.

"So, we get you, Simon. We've also faced backlash for our work. But you know what, we're influencers. Sometimes you have to be willing to take risks for the people you influence." And that was as close to an admission as Jenna Lang would ever come to acknowledging that documenting their trip into a restricted wilderness was no accident. She knew it would rile up plenty of Minnesotans, and knew that it would result in more clicks on their videos. The growth of their audience was worth one-hundred-fold of what they paid in fines for their exploits. They were no journalists, but they did know social media. And more than anything, they wanted a national audience.

It was Jana's turn to jump in. "OK. Simon, enough of the hard-hitting stuff, let's get to why you're here today. Tell us about the jelly and peanut butter sandwich. It sounds pretty simple. Why have I never heard of it?"

"That's a great question, Jana. You would think in this day and age that we've seen it all, but every once in a generation someone thinks of food in such a unique way that it changes the way we think about food pairings altogether. I was on a trip with some college friends to El Grain, Wisconsin."

"El Grain? What about El Grain made you go there?"

"You know, it was a bit of a reunion with some college friends. We were camping. And then, I guess you could say I just felt this calling to stop in El Grain. I just have a nose for these things. It's a gift; I'm so blessed." Ignoring plenty of details, Simon continued.

"We stopped at this place called Miss Betty's Diner. Cute little place. Undiscovered. No social media presence. Hardly any reviews, but I knew we had to stop. My friends ordered pretty traditional stuff: burgers, pot pies, you know. But I was drawn to this new sandwich. She calls it a jelly and peanut butter sandwich and that's what it is. It's so simple, but we're going to put her on the map today. When you get to El Grain, stop at Miss Betty's Diner. I may have discovered her, but she's the real star."

"Let's say we can't get to El Grain anytime soon. I understand you can help us make one of these sandwiches on our own. Is that true?"

"Absolutely."

"Great. And we will do just that right after this commercial break."

After the break Simon walked them through making a jelly and peanut butter sandwich. To make the segment feel more complete and enhance his standing as an expert, he shared how the simplest iteration of sandwich had many variations. He talked through all of the various jams and jellies one could use. He discussed the difference made by using creamy versus chunky peanut butter. And he was most excited to share how different breads changed the sandwich profile and mouthfeel. He reserved his most excitement for his final announcement.

"Jenna, Jana, I've never done this before, but this sandwich has me so excited that I recommended it to the Sammies for consideration as Best Sandwich of the Year. And I just heard back from them yesterday—so you're hearing it here first. The jelly and peanut butter sandwich from Miss Betty's Diner is an official nominee for Sandwich of the Year. For only the second time ever, a Wisconsin restaurant may win a coveted Sammie."

"Wow. That is breaking news, folks! How did Miss Betty react to the news?"

"Oh. I haven't talked to her about this... I bet the people at the Sammies will reach out to her. You know what, that's a really good point."

6—On Podcasters

Joshua was pleased that his mother was finally getting the recognition she deserved. At her request, he was taking a bit of time off of work to be with her up in El Grain. When the segment on jelly and peanut butter sandwiches aired on television, a slow-building wave of popularity gathered more water. First, there had been the locals and their love-hate relationship with the new people visiting their town.

"Betty, who knew a sandwich could bring you so much popularity? I'll have to try one of those new sandwiches."

"Oh, I suppose you'll be getting too famous for the likes of our town now, won't you?"

"I hope your fame won't be bringing too many folks to our town."

"I haven't seen this much publicity in our town since, what, the early nineties? Is that when the gentlemen's club opened up?"

A few locals did find it odd that they ran a whole segment on Miss Betty's Diner without a single quote from the creator of the sandwich being discussed. Plenty of news outlets felt the same way, and the wave continued to grow. The race was on to see who could score the first interview with Miss Betty. After the segment aired on *Twin Cities Twins*, it was picked up nationally by a feel-good evening infotainment program. From there, the daytime and late night shows got involved. Drew Barrymore figured it would be a great fit for her audience. Jimmy Fallon felt the same. This was part of the reason that Betty asked Joshua to help her out.

"Mom, I think you should do it. Why not enjoy your fifteen minutes?"

"Joshua, the only thing I did was put jelly and peanut butter onto a couple of pieces of bread. I can't believe I'm the first person to do this. You're all making too big a deal out of a sandwich made to placate picky eight-year-olds."

"Then say that. Go on Colbert and tell him that. It's endearing."

"I don't know about being on TV."

"Then do a podcast. Everyone's got one these days. I bet that just today you had two or three customers who are going to podcast about their experience at Miss Betty's Diner. They probably have an audience of twelve people, but it's already happening. You may as well find one you feel good about and do an interview. I know how much you put into raising me and giving me every opportunity to succeed. You could really parlay this exposure to get you closer to retirement."

"Who says I'm retiring?"

"Fine. You could use the extra money to travel more."

"How does an interview make extra money?"

"More customers, for one thing. We can talk more about this later. Can I at least look through the list of podcast interview requests for you?"

"Sure, but I'm not promising anything. My current staff is already taxed. I don't know how much more business we can handle right now. And about these podcasts, you don't have to explain them to me. Back in the early nineties the movie *Pump Up the Volume* prophesied a world where everyone could broadcast their own voice. Only the vehicle wasn't Spotify, but pirate radio. If I remember right, things didn't end so well. Or maybe they did. I don't know, it's been over thirty years."

"I imagine things are a bit different now than some Gen X Ethan Hawke movie."

"That's Christian Slater, young man. Steal the air. Talk hard."

"What?"

"It's from the movie. Never mind."

+ + + + +

Soon after that, Betty Einfach found herself as a guest on *Chi-Town Foodie*. She still wasn't certain that she wanted to do an interview, but she trusted her son even if he didn't know the difference between Ethan Hawke and Christian Slater. They had worked through at least a dozen other options before landing on the popular podcaster committed to the Midwestern food scene.

As expected, Betty turned down all of Joshua's television options. He was, in effect, acting as her agent in this process. As time wore on, he took a formal leave from his work in Milwaukee to help his mother. He was in a fortunate position to be able to do so, and he rather liked this new role. There were immediate options on either coast, but Betty waffled on whether or not she wanted to travel there. Soon those shows lost interest in favor of their pursuit to land the driving chimpanzee story in Nebraska.

A man from Kearney, Nebraska, claimed that his chimpanzee drove him to the emergency department of his local hospital as he was suffering a cardiac episode. The man's story fell apart under the slightest scrutiny but it was entertaining. Thomas McGintry did have a history of atrial fibrillation, and the chimpanzee was in the driver's seat, that much was true. However, Tom was enrolled in a self-driving car experiment and the hospital was a pre-set location to test whether the car could provide a quicker and more efficient response than an ambulance. No doctor would confirm that Tom was in A-fib when he arrived at the ER, and he wasn't admitted to the hospital, stating that his condition had corrected itself by the time he arrived there. When pressed by the hard-hitting journalism of Jimmy Kimmel he admitted that he made the whole thing up because he didn't want to lose possession of his beloved chimp, Ensom. The lonely chap had taken the chimp from a faltering zoo in California and moved back home to Nebraska. Ignoring regulations regarding exotic pets, he created a preposterous situation whereby he could claim his pet not only provided emotional support, but protected his very life. What started as a feel-good story about a chimpanzee saving a man's life by driving him to the hospital became a sad tale of a lonely man devoid of any meaningful human relationships.

Betty reminded Joshua that this was precisely why she didn't want to appear on national TV. After switching focus to podcasts, she again eschewed any options for huge audiences from equally large cities, until they came across *Chi-Town Foodie*. Shawn Kramer ran the podcast from his home office in Naperville. When his show made it to fifty episodes he knew that he was in the top one percent of all podcasts. His audience didn't compare to celebrity offerings, but he knew he was a rare podcaster who made money in this field. He loved talking about food from across Chicagoland, and he was relentlessly mocked by those from Chicago-proper for his suburban take on the Chicago food scene. Nevertheless, he powered through, turning haters into fans with his relentless enthusiasm. He surprised many with his take on deep dish pizza when he named Pequod's as the best in the city. Betty had done her homework and this was who she wanted to talk to—if she had to talk with anyone.

+ + + + +

"Today on *Chi-Town Foodie*, we're traveling north through the cheddar curtain to check out a new sandwich. Welcome, Betty Einfach, owner of Miss Betty's Diner in El Grain, Wisconsin."

"Thank you Shawn. I hope you enjoy your time in our town."

"Yes, as many of you know, I typically record from my home studio, but in this instance, Betty's very insistent manager convinced me to come to El Grain to truly experience the jelly and peanut butter sandwich in its native home."

"That was my son, Joshua. He knows my reluctance to do media interviews."

"And thankful we are to be your first media interview since your sandwich has recently gone viral. And, while we've only known of it for a short time, how long have you been making jelly and peanut butter sandwiches?"

"I suppose I put them in Joshua's lunches when he was in elementary school. So, at least twenty years, I guess?"

"Really, you could put peanut butter in a school lunch?"

"It was a different time."

"So, this sandwich has survived in anonymity for twenty years and we're just learning about it now?"

"I guess so. I really don't see it as anything special. It's really just three ingredients. The fuss seems a bit much, but I'm glad people like it."

"The fuss is that you are up for Sandwich of the Year. Don't undersell your contribution to the ever-changing food scene."

It was a good conversation with Shawn. He was a good listener. Asked sharp questions and made her feel at home—which proved that it was a good choice to make the trip to El Grain. She convinced herself that Shawn was just another one of Joshua's friends. She talked to him like she talked to Brady. She felt so good about it that she gave Joshua the go-ahead to book another interview. Her trust in Joshua was well placed. Even he couldn't have seen what would happen in Nashville.

7—On the Use of Trademark Law

"Good morning, Nashville. I'm your host, Imogene Wilder, and y'all, we've got a great show for you this morning. You know we love our neighborly family to the north, and we've got a special visitor from those stompin' grounds with us today."

It's true. For some reason, Nashville and Milwaukee make good partners. The Milwaukee Admirals serve as an affiliate for the NHL's Nashville Predators. Likewise, the Nashville Sounds are the AAA affiliate for the Milwaukee Brewers. We'll leave it to the sociologists to figure out why else this odd couple of cities feel like kindred spirits, for it's well beyond the scope of this here kitchen fable.

"Welcome to Nashville, Betty Einfach. Did I say that right?"

"That was just fine, Imogene. I'm happy to be here."

The first segment had a nice mother-daughter-type feel. They didn't break a lot of new ground, but it was new information to this Nashville audience, so Betty took her time explaining the history of her sandwich, the news story in Minneapolis, the podcast in Chicago, and now her first television exposure. And, like many mother-daughter relationships, Imogene and Betty were about to experience a strained interaction.

"Welcome back, everyone. I'm sitting down with Betty Einfach, of Miss Betty's Diner in El Grain, Wisconsin. Betty, we've loved hearing about how you created the jelly and peanut butter sandwich. Of course, we've cherished the peanut butter and banana sandwich made famous by Elvis for years, but who knew? Jelly? That's wild."

"I guess I use wild berries sometimes, but Imogene, like I've told everyone else, it's really not a complicated sandwich. I don't understand the big fuss."

"Oh, Betty, don't be so modest. Your sandwich is the talk of the town. Let me share some of the places where your story is making news…

"A Palo Alto school district had to issue a special bulletin banning jelly and peanut butter sandwiches in school lunches. It was just an extension of the existing nut ban, but apparently too many parents were flouting the embargo, opting for the beautiful simplicity of your sandwich.

"From the Kennedy Space Center, next month, astronaut Kelly Markkuson is taking a jelly and peanut butter sandwich into space, intending to eat the sandwich once in orbit.

"Weird Al Yankovic claims that he is working on a sandwich parody song. He didn't disclose the source material, but he was seen talking to Lady Gaga's lawyers so people are speculating wildly as to which song he may be using.

"Congressman Bill Richter entered the jelly and peanut butter sandwich into the congressional record as he ate a sandwich while using it as a metaphor for much needed bipartisanship.

"I've also heard rumors that both Netflix and Prime have approached you about turning the story of your sandwich into a mini-series. Is there any truth to that?"

Having finally been given a chance to interject, Betty offered, "Imogene, that all sounds like nonsense, but I once heard it said that 'a little nonsense now and then is relished by the wisest men,' so maybe I should just enjoy the nonsense."

"Is that a movie quote?"

"Perhaps, and given your name, I'm not surprised that it resonates with you."

"Ooh. So mysterious, but I need to move on because there is one more story that I need to share with you and get your input." Imogene lacked the curiosity to pursue the source of that quote any further. Plus, she had something else on her mind.

34

She steeled herself, took a deep breath, and knew that this was her opportunity. She'd run the line a dozen times looking for the right mix of intrigue, compassion, and seriousness—and so she began.

"Betty, this last one brings me no pleasure, but there's a man backstage. Yesterday he gave me this letter and asked me to pass it along to you during our interview. I'll give it to you in a moment, but Betty, this is a cease-and-desist letter from Ted Wellington. He claims that he is the rightful creator of the jelly and peanut butter sandwich. He says that he has made sandwiches of jelly and peanut butter since childhood and he's loved them ever since. Further, he says that he never intended to file a trademark, but seeing you profit off of his sandwich, he filed for trademark protection for the name 'Jelly and Peanut Butter Sandwich' last month and is awaiting approval of his application. Do you have any response?"

An ounce of recognition raced across Betty's mind before she calmly responded, "Oh, Imogene, you don't need to worry. I've said from the very beginning that it's just a simple sandwich. I'm sure that Ted isn't the only one who ever made this sandwich. Anyone should feel free to make a jelly and peanut butter sandwich."

"Betty, I'm not sure you understand what this letter is demanding. Let me bring out our special guest, and he can describe the full content of the letter. Ladies and gentlemen, please welcome Mr. Theodore Wellington."

"Good morning, Imogene. Betty. I am thankful for this opportunity to set the record straight, and sorry that it had to come to this."

Off stage, Joshua felt his stomach drop. What was going on here? He wasn't sure, but he needed it to stop. He wasn't proud of it, but he did the only thing he could think of. He walked up to the cameraman, grabbed his headset, and started yelling, "Go to commercial. Go to commercial," into the microphone.

Both Joshua and Imogene approached each other with the same question. "What the hell was that?"

Imogene went first. "This is a live television show. You can't just interrupt its progress. Security is on their way to escort you out."

"If I'm leaving, my mother is coming with me. What kind of stunt is this? You never mentioned any of this."

"It's television, Joshua. It's pretty common to have more than one guest. I don't see why you're upset. I'm looking forward to a nice conversation between Ted and Betty."

"No. You're looking to create a spectacle; to record snippets of video that get posted far and wide so you can enhance your future opportunities."

"You're not wrong, but you're mistaken if you think any of this will make your mom look bad. Who do you think will look sympathetic to our audience in this situation? Your demure mother, or the billionaire who's trying to trademark a sandwich name?" Turning her attention, she continued in Ted's direction, "I'm sorry, Ted, but it's true."

"Of course, but I have the law on my side so let's get the conversation started."

Betty pulled Joshua off to the side for a little consultation.

"It's just a sandwich, Joshua. I don't understand why you're getting worked up."

"Mom. I'm angry because I feel terrible. You didn't want to do this in the first place and now it's a whole debacle. Let's leave."

"I don't mind talking to Mr. Wellington."

"No. I've seen his type before. He has no interest in creating anything new. He's just looking for a way to monetize someone else's work."

"Well, making money's not a bad thing. Remember, you were encouraging something similar not too long ago. Make some money, Mom. Work towards retirement, Mom. Do some traveling... Remember that?"

"Of course I remember that. That's why I said I know the Ted Wellingtons of the world. I am him. Do you know I've had more fun trying to turn your idea into money than I've had in years practicing family law? It's a terrible confession, and I hate that I feel that way. You are creative and free. I can't let you become like us."

"Oh, Joshua, I know your heart. C'mon. Let's go grab some hot chicken and talk it out. This wave has been building for a while. It's about time it crested."

8—On the Celebration of Sammies

It would be right to assume that some time passed between Betty's trip to Nashville and the Sammie Awards. How much time is not important because, remember, this is not a documentary. It is perhaps convenient for this work-shy storyteller that fables need not follow a strict sense of time.

"Good evening, ladies and gentlemen, I am Verne Lawlor, and welcome to the Thirteenth Annual Sammie Awards, where we celebrate all things that can be stuffed between two pieces of bread."

The Sammies, as they are known, started as a tongue-in-cheek event following the American Culinary Awards, which celebrate the finest in dining experiences across America. Awards include Best Entree, Best Young Chef, Exceptional Achievement in Ambience, and the coveted Best Restaurant Award. Over the years, a clever marketing team made the awards into the premier event for the celebration of food. It began when the board of directors lured the executive director from the Westminster Dog Show to take on the challenge. They wanted casual observers to tune in; they wanted to be the Kentucky Derby of dining, the Tony Awards of fine food, the Wimbledon of wine pairings—and they had succeeded. Over decades they had grown from a celebration for industry insiders into a red carpet gastronomical gala. And, as respect for the event grew, so did the pretense. Restaurant owners became celebrities, wooing appraisers with free meals. Chefs became rock stars, using their award speeches to politic for their platform—whether it be world hunger or plant-based eating.

Yet, each and every year, after the awards had been distributed, guests by the dozens descended on the twenty-four-hour diner across the street from the Pacific Theatre in Los Angeles to eat at Earl's. Mere minutes after they finished a grandiloquent celebration of The State and Wells Club's A5 Wagyu Filet Mignon, many would be enjoying a burger, fries, and chocolate shake. The hypocrisy of it all bothered the diner's owner, and while he was not the Earl of Sandwich, he was a guy named Earl who made some pretty good sandwiches.

He was bothered enough that Earl started his own counter-programming to the American Culinary Awards. He dubbed it The Sammies, with each winner receiving a trophy and free sandwiches whenever they were in town for a visit. Celebrating the food that regular people eat on a daily basis, the rules are simple. If it's food that fits between slices of bread, it is eligible to be recognized. The first year's winner was a five-cheese grilled cheese with a single tomato slice from Madison, Wisconsin. Up until now, it was the only Midwestern sandwich to win a Sammie. The Maid-Rite from Iowa was a runner-up one year, but it was hard to believe that not a single sandwich from Illinois, Indiana, Ohio, Pennsylvania, or Michigan had won. Philly Cheesesteak—nothing. Chicago hot dog—nothing, perhaps due to the debate of whether or not a hot dog truly was a sandwich. A Polish boy from Ohio—nothing, perhaps due to the same problem. A Minnesota Walleye sandwich—nothing. Big Jane's BBQ Joint from Kansas City did win for their Burnt Ends Sandwich, and that's about as close to a Midwestern winner as you could find.

Meanwhile, the East Coast was well represented with the Rising Tides lobster roll from Maine, Ellicott City Diner's crab cake sandwich from Maryland, and Cajun's muffuletta from New York City. California and Texas each boasted three winners. The Bayou's Po-Boy won for Louisiana, and Down the Hatch, a hatch chili quesadilla from Red Rocks in New Mexico, rounded out all the past winners.

Year thirteen finally brought some finalists from the Midwest, and given the surging popularity of jelly and peanut butter sandwiches, followers of the award were certain that it was time for a second winner from Wisconsin to make its mark.

While the crowd across the street salivated over the description of a pomegranate and honey-glazed duck with rice, the assembly at Earl's ate samples from all of the nominees. To Earl's thinking, words don't activate taste buds. It was better to taste and smell than to hear about how good the food was. Served like a flight of beer at the local brewery, each attendee received a quarter sandwich of the four nominees for Sandwich of the Year. And, even though this was intended to be an irreverent response to the culinary awards, over the past twelve years Earl had cleverly turned the event into a viral occasion for the streaming age.

"As many of you know, Earl and I grew up as neighbors from the southern suburbs of Chicago. He was taking orders from the time he was nine years old at his folks' place, the Tinley Park Confectionary. I was always broke and hungry and his family took care of me. I ate more meals at their restaurant than I did at home. So, when they relocated to LA, of course I joined them. Earl's been the kindest man I know and in true fashion, all of the money raised here tonight will go to the Meals for Children Task Force. It's my honor to be your emcee so let's get on with the awards.

"We've got about an hour before the ACA folks descend on us, hungry for burgers and fries, so let's not waste any time. The nominees for Best Use of Bacon are..."

+ + + + +

Joshua and Betty were seated in the middle of the dining room at Earl's. After the hubbub at the podcast with the cease-and-desist letter, Joshua was reticent to have his mother do any more public events. He felt terrible. She was unbothered. For as much as she didn't understand the fuss of celebrating a jelly and peanut butter sandwich, she was taking the whole idea in stride. Joshua was even a bit surprised by how good of a traveler she was. She ably navigated the Minneapolis airport and even looked comfortable getting through LAX. She rolled her small carry-on following the signs to the car service, and easily threw her bag into the back of their Uber. Joshua was impressed. He'd always thought of his mom as a small-town girl resistant to the big city. She reminded him that she had a life before he was born and actually had done some pretty regular traveling between eighteen and twenty-eight years old. It was a period she didn't discuss often, and Joshua wanted to know more. Her response to his inquiry was to ask him if he was willing to tell all of his escapades during his college years. She concluded that line of questioning by letting Joshua know that they didn't have to know all of each other's actions to fully love each other.

Joshua couldn't help but think about the idea that his mother had a life before him. He'd only known her as a diner owner. Even during the social hour before the awards show began he was amazed at how she socialized with other restaurateurs. There was a playfulness, almost a flirting nature that he had never recognized. Here he thought he needed to protect his mother from the big-city folk in Chicago and LA. How wrong he'd been. In talking with Big John of Top's Diner in Chicago it was mere minutes before the two were talking like old friends. They commiserated about their favorite type of customer, the challenge of finding good servers, and the loss of revenue to credit card fees. If anything, the creation of this new sandwich was causing Joshua to see his mother in a new light. He'd always been proud of her. He always respected her. He always loved her. And, even though the word fell short, he found himself admiring her. When they took their seats, he said as much.

"Mom, after the podcast debacle, I thought I was being selfish to make you come out here for the Sammies. But you kind of like this, don't you?"

"Oh, Joshua, it's all a bit much for slapping peanut butter and jelly between two slices of bread, but these other deli owners; we're of the same ilk. We like to feed people and we like to observe people. I've always enjoyed talking to other restaurant owners. And, whether you're in a big city or a small town, you end up having a group of regulars who become your community. I chose a small town. We can talk more later, but since we're here let's have some fun."

+ + + + +

Verne was back at the microphone, having given the second to last award of the night to Trish's Drive-In. Their chili cheeseburger had just earned the coveted award for Best Taste, Worst Mess.

"Congratulations, Trish. There's a reason they're a drive-in, people. Turn off the ignition and stay awhile. You do not want to try and eat that sandwich while driving. Now, we're going to take a brief moment for the servers to bring you all plates of our nominees for this year's top prize, Sandwich of the Year. And, as a reminder, if we see any of you posting photos of these sandwiches on Insta, you will be banned from next year's event. We're celebrating taste here tonight, folks. We do not give awards based on presentation. So put those phones away. That comes from Earl himself.

"OK. Let's take a look at the sandwiches before you. First up, let's talk about how peanut butter is on our list twice tonight. From Amherst, Massachusetts, Bell's has been bringing food to this college town for decades. This is their second nomination and first in this category. I'll invite you now to take a bite of the fluffernutter sandwich on your plate. As you eat, let me tell you that this marks the first time that a sandwich with marshmallow has been a finalist for sandwich of the year. I don't know if marshmallow crème was invented in Massachusetts, but over one hundred years ago it became known as fluff when Archibald Query sold his recipe to candymakers Durkee and Mower. Many a New England child has been known to eat this sandwich in their school lunch while trying to figure out how Randy Moss never won a Super Bowl with the Patriots. And, if you laughed at that, I'll assume that you are not a millennial or younger.

"Second on our list of sandwiches tonight is the Italian beef sandwich from Top's in Midlothian, Illinois. Hey, that's my old stomping grounds. Where are you at, Big John? Good to see you. Welcome to the Sammies. You're making Chicago proud tonight."

THE KITCHEN FABLE

Recognizing that he was showing partiality, Verne caught himself.

"Oh boy, is my favoritism showing? Rest easy, everyone, Earl tells me that we've got accountants and everything who tally all the votes. There will be no shenanigans when it comes to the winner. OK, now that I cleared that up, let me tell you what's on the Italian beef. Top's makes their sandwich with the traditional hero roll that's soaked in the juices of the thinly sliced beef. On top of that there's a proprietary, house-made blend of pickled vegetables. Top's eschews the modern addition of provolone and keeps it simple.

"Third on our list comes a vegetarian banh mi sandwich from the Riverside Deli in Snohomish, Washington. They marinade the tofu for twenty-four hours, add some tangy mayonnaise, with pickled carrots and cucumbers, diced cilantro, and put it all on a crunchy baguette. And there you have a Vietnamese classic. You know, I'm getting the sense that pickled veggies on sandwiches are really having their moment. Sometimes, to make great tastes you can't rush the process. Which brings us to our final nominee for Sandwich of the Year—and this one you can make in a hurry.

"From Miss Betty's Diner in El Grain, Wisconsin, we've got a brand new sandwich. I'm told that a name change is under consideration, so we'll just call it a jelly *with* peanut butter sandwich. Miss Betty takes two slices of homemade cottage bread and spreads some homemade peanut butter. Betty, do you really make your peanut butter at the diner? I'm getting a nod, so you see, that's what you get out of these Sammie Awards. It's the little extra bits of effort that really elevate these awards to the next level. And then Betty adds jelly to the sandwich. It looks like she sources her jams and jellies from local makers in Wisconsin, strengthening the local economy.

"Fantastic. I hope you've had a chance to sample all four of these sandwiches by now. If not, too bad, because we're moving on to the winner. May I have the envelope and winner's sandwich, please?"

Verne wasted no time seeing that Earl had given him the signal to wrap it up.

"Tonight's winner goes home with the pride of having won the Sammie for Sandwich of the Year, a 3-D printed trophy, made by Earl's niece in her college's engineering lab, and never again will the winner have to pay for a Dagwood at Earl's. Anytime you're in town, you can eat for free. Hey, winners, you can be just like me—freeloading off of Earl for years to come."

Earl's niece was an engineer back in the Midwest where he still had family. She ran the maker space at Frederick College in Central Illinois. There weren't a lot of aspiring female engineers when she was growing up, so she had trouble fitting in. She always loved her summer visits to see Uncle Earl. She was always true to herself in the Chicago suburbs, but she felt less anxiety about it when she was in LA. Most of it was Uncle Earl and Aunt Mimi, part of it was the neighborhood where they lived, and the rest of it was simply the anonymity of being in a new place. After her senior year, she spent the summer as a server at Earl's. She found a new confidence through the daily interactions with these people she would never see again. She always thought she was an introvert. It turned out she was just shy. She learned about her need to be around people, and she took this knowledge into her studies as a future engineer. Eternally grateful for the world that Earl and Mimi helped her discover, she seized the opportunity to help when she first heard about the Sammies. Designing a prototype on her laptop, she sent it to the 3-D printer. Once rendered, she sent the sample to Earl. The shape was half of a grilled cheese sandwich with a single bite taken out of the middle of the cut edge. Opposite the bite mark was a hole for a pin to attach it to a trophy base. She imagined a full-color version that would highlight the grill marks on the bread and the oozing cheese. Earl loved it, without the embellishments. He said the prototype reminded him of the plastic animals from the Mold-A-Rama at the Brookfield Zoo that he used to buy as a kid. Thirteen years later, Becky Reisen still used the same design and lab to produce all of Earl's Sammie Awards. Earl made sure to pay both Becky and the college for their work.

"Without further ado, this year's winner of Sandwich of the Year goes to... Miss Betty's Diner, for her jelly and peanut butter sandwich. Congratulations, Betty. Come on up and you've got thirty seconds to say something nice before we open the doors to welcome others."

As Betty took the microphone a man quickly pushed his way through the crowd and grabbed the microphone from her hand.

"Betty, I'ma let you finish, but as the owner of the trademark for the jelly and peanut butter sandwich, I wanted to say thank you for recognizing this sandwich that I created well before Miss Betty made it famous."

Verne didn't take kindly to Ted Wellington's interruption and hip-checked him to the ground while securing the microphone and passing it to Betty for a second time. Betty shared her gratitude while Verne ushered Ted to the exit. Betty saw what was happening and offered an olive branch.

"Verne, Ted can stay. I'm really thankful for the chance to be with all of you enterprising people tonight. If I've learned something in my years running a diner, it's that we've got to support each other. I don't understand trademarks, copyrights, or patents, but I know that anyone can go home tonight and slap some jelly and peanut butter on a couple of slices of bread. Ted, I'm sure you make wonderful sandwiches. It sounds like we both wanted to find a tasty, cost-effective way to feed people. Why don't you stick around and we can celebrate together?"

"No. It's clear that I'm not wanted here tonight. It's also clear that this is a violation of the cease-and-desist letter you were served. You'll be hearing from my lawyers. Enjoy the victory while it lasts. You may have won Sandwich of the Year, but you've served your last jelly and peanut butter sandwich."

Part Two

9—On the Origins of the Rogue Collective

For Joshua's eleventh birthday, Betty let Joshua host an overnight with some of his friends. She assumed it would be a gaggle of pre-pubescent boys, content to play video games and watch a couple of movies. She was a bit surprised when the only two friends who showed up were Brady and Penny. Concerned that he was encountering some social problems at school, she pulled him aside to ask how he felt about only two friends showing up.

When he gave her a quizzical look she asked, "Joshua, did you invite anyone else?"

"No. I told you I wanted an overnight with my friends. These are my friends."

"Well, surely you have more friends than Brady and Penny."

"Yeah, but not overnight friends."

That evening, Betty learned that Joshua was happy to be friends with just about anyone, but overnight friends were special. They were the people that he could handle for fifteen hours straight. Only two people met that criteria.

Once Betty realized that there would only be two friends at the overnight, she let her guard down. Brady and Penny were in the apartment all the time. For crying out loud, they called her Mom Betty. So comfortable was she that she went to bed at 10 p.m., telling the kids to behave and try to get some sleep. Neither of those suggestions sounded overly appealing. They waited until 11:30 to sneak down to the diner. There they had a choice to make. They could sneak out the back door and risk making enough noise that Betty would wake up. The other option was to use the front door.

It was farther from the apartment and less likely to wake Betty, but it also meant they would be leaving the diner unlocked for any passersby. The choice was obvious. Don't risk waking up mom.

"Don't forget the bucket," Penny whispered to Brady.

"Duh. I'm not an idiot."

"I don't know, Brady. You did come to an overnight without a sleeping bag," Josh jumped in.

"Why carry something I'm not going to use?"

"Shhh. Don't wake Mom Betty."

After a typical mini-spat, the three of them safely escaped the front door of Miss Betty's Diner, narrowly avoiding the gaze of first-year policeman Officer Gary Nealy. Joshua and Brady each carried a bucket of balloons while Penny carried the launchers. Their intent was to hide behind the sign of St. Bernard's Catholic Church and launch balloons at cars traveling down Second Street, which oddly was the main street through town. They were convinced that the launchers would allow them to stay hidden while still being able to reach the cars passing by.

For his part, Joshua had filled up his balloons with a shaving cream and water concoction. He got the idea from a new video-sharing site called YouTube. He was supposed to be using the school computer for history research, but the allure of online videos was strong even back in 2006. It was a good thing for Joshua that the school was not yet monitoring the search histories of students.

Brady, on the other hand, went with a bucket of traditional water balloons. Nothing fancy, just a nice splash on the windshield. He did embellish a few of the balloons by taping feathers to them. In his eleven-year-old mind he thought it would be funny for people to think that they'd just crushed a poor little bird.

Penny didn't have an opinion on the water balloons. She only wanted to make sure that they focused on hitting cars that deserved to get hit. How exactly they were going to determine that was uncertain, but it was important to her. Brady argued that anyone out at midnight probably deserved it. Joshua warned that they may want to avoid any trucks that looked like they would be hell-bent on tracking down the culprits. Again, how they would determine those people was a matter they could not solve.

After a lengthy discussion about launch angles, they were ready to attempt the first launch. Joshua wanted to go first since it was his birthday. The others agreed. For the sake of staying hidden, he decided to launch it from behind the sign at a nice high angle. They guessed at how long it would take to reach the cars passing by. Once they were all set, Penny gave a countdown—Three—Two—One—Launch. Splat. The shaving cream and water balloon exploded on the church sign, failing to clear the one obstacle in its way. The explosion hit all of them equally and triggered a tsunami of laughter from the would be pranksters.

"You've got to launch it higher!"

"No. I think we need to step to the side so it doesn't hit the sign."

"But that'll leave the shooter exposed."

"Not if they duck behind the sign once they launch it."

"Fine. Let's give it another try, but use a regular balloon this time."

Having recalibrated their angles like the sharpshooters they were, Brady launched a second balloon, overshooting the road entirely, landing on the far sidewalk. The consolation was that it did provide a nice explosion. Now they just needed to work on distance. Balloon after balloon they got better at hitting the street. They still hadn't hit anything... except the church sign and themselves. They learned that the water balloons traveled farther than the shaving cream balloons. They learned that they were waiting too long to launch the balloons. Sooner or later they would hit their mark. With such a steep learning curve, they had given up on trying to hit the perfect car. Where once they would've loved to hit an open convertible—a unicorn in the town of El Grain—they now would be satisfied with hitting any car at all.

It was Joshua's turn again. He lined up his shot. Penny let him know when she saw the headlights of an approaching vehicle. This time it was an older model pickup truck with visible rust around the wheel wells. It was the type of vehicle that earlier in the night they would've avoided. Perhaps it would've been wise to keep that rule in place. Three—Two—One—Launch. The balloon made a beautiful arc through the night sky. Was this it? They all took a peek around the church sign. It was glorious. A direct hit on the passenger side of the windshield. The driver immediately stepped on the brakes, no doubt surprised by the attack. The kids ducked behind the church sign, both giggling and nervous. Sneaking a peek, they watched the truck drive off. Once clear, the innocent laughter of pre-teens filled the night air, never realizing how truly reckless their behavior was.

They were too giddy to make any other successful launches. They made a couple of half-hearted efforts, but soon they began to tire and were debating what to do with the leftover balloons. None of them immediately noticed the imposing figure approaching in the dark. Penny was the first to see him.

"Guys. Shut up!"

"What?"

"Shut up!" There was a nervousness in her voice. Brady and Josh turned toward her and spied the terrifying face looking at them. He said nothing. His mere presence was enough to instill a sense of fear that none of them had ever felt before.

"Are you a cop?" No response.

"Do you know what we're doing?" No response.

"I'm so sorry. We're just playing a silly game. Can we just go home now?" Finally a response.

"Tell me about this game."

They quickly realized that the man standing before them was not just out on a late-night walk, but was indeed the man whose truck they christened with a shaving cream bath. He had them all take a seat on the church steps where he had them explain everything about what they were doing. A 1 a.m. confessional on the church steps with Osmo Laasinen was enough to put nearly anyone on the straight and narrow. Osmo was a semi-retired professor from Eisleben College in town. He was also known as a bit of a recluse since his daughter died. What the kids didn't know was that Osmo was in the midst of his own brand of vigilante justice so he needed to keep things moving with these kids. And, while it's an entertaining tale of Osmo chastising a useless insurance claims adjustor, as previously mentioned, we shan't follow every tangential story no matter how tantalizing it may be.

"So, how do you pick your victims?"

Joshua felt compelled to answer. "We had a rule to only launch balloons at those who looked like they deserved it."

"And I looked like that to you?"

Shoot. That sounded bad. "Well, Penny had an idea…" Nope. He didn't want to drag her into this. "It turns out we weren't very good. So we tried to hit anything we could."

"I see… So, you're a fine little collection of rogues, but you're missing something. You need a code of conduct."

With that, Moose, as his friends called him, taught the kids about the proper way to misbehave. First, your victims shall not be chosen at random. A proper victim is not a victim at all, but someone who has earned payment for their behavior. Second, the payment has to fit the offense. If someone steals shaving cream from the local drug store, then a shaving cream balloon to the face is a fitting response. Third, it is fine if the payment inconveniences the perpetrator, but it shouldn't routinely bear a significant financial cost. Fourth, using misbehavior to bully someone is never proper. And, finally, you should always have plausible deniability for whatever action you take. It is fine for the perpetrator to know it is you, but they must not be able to prove it.

"If you can follow these rules, your misbehavior will feel purposeful instead of just dangerous. You're all lucky that I am sick and running late, otherwise you'd be using that shaving cream to shave your heads. Do you understand?"

They all nodded. Was this really all the punishment they were going to receive?

"I suggest you head home now. I'm sure you mother is worried sick. She's probably awake back at the diner." He was letting them go, but he knew who they were. They understood.

They gathered their belongings and hustled back to the diner, saying nothing until Brady broke the silence. "Did you hear that? He called us a collection of rogues."

+ + + + +

"Is it really possible that in the last three months your mom created a new sandwich, won best sandwich of the year, and is now being sued for it?"

For the second time in three months, the trio of Brady Samuels, Penelope Barnes, and Joshua Einfach were enjoying each other's company. Having traded a campsite on the Mississippi for a table at the Indigo Blue coffee shop, the three friends were pondering how, in a strange way, a hungry raccoon bore at least some of the responsibility for all that transpired.

It began with Brady's idea for a thirtieth-birthday campout. Betty's only role was doing what came naturally—providing food for her kid and his friends. The raccoon was also doing what came naturally—seeking fattening foods as the weather turned colder. For her part, Penny had offered up the sandwiches to the hungry campers. Simon, one of those campers, bore the lion's share of responsibility, having used the encounter to build on his own brand. And Joshua had encouraged his mother to take ownership of the narrative when the snowball of attention started rolling down the hill. Of course, all of these events were further enabled by the consumption behavior of modern Americans. With eyes glued to smartphones, ever scrolling for satisfaction, Betty's concoction provided a simple solution to feeding hungry people. The matter remained unsettled whether her sandwich of jelly and peanut butter was capable of feeding those starving souls.

Joshua was busy trying to help his mother with the nuisance lawsuit filed by Ted Wellington. His firm offered minimal resistance when he asked to open a satellite office back in his home town, yet he was advised that this unusual request may delay his window for becoming a partner. It was a possibility that he was willing to accept. He was currently splitting time between the diner and his mom's place, but in the new year there was a small office available next to the town dentist. He didn't want to be around long enough to sign a lease, but he was already getting swamped with business. His mother and friends put out word that he was open to taking on clients. That was enough to keep his phone buzzing. Some people needed a will, one woman needed help settling her parents' estate, another needed representation for his divorce proceedings and custody battle. Finally, poor Eileen Bremerton, mere months from retirement, had mixed up her medications and woke up in her seventh-grade pre-algebra classroom wearing only a nightgown as students began filing in for the day. Video footage confirmed that she had driven into the flagpole with her 2004 Toyota Camry at 4:30 a.m. and headed straight to her classroom. After being treated at the hospital for a concussion, abrasions from the airbag, and ridding the drugs from her system, she was advised to get a lawyer. The cops didn't know what charges to pursue, for the otherwise sober woman was a beloved community member having taught every child at the El Grain middle school for the last forty years. Knowing they couldn't ignore someone driving into the flagpole outside of a school, the responding deputy secretly hoped that Joshua would find them an off-ramp to quietly put this issue to rest.

With sparse free time to renew dormant high school friendships, Joshua focused most of his idle hours on his mother or his friends Brady and Penny.

"Can I tell you both how much I learned about my mom on our trips to Nashville and Los Angeles this fall? I always had this vision of her as a small-town single mom, caring for me at the expense of her own happiness. Meanwhile I was the kid who left town for the city. I know that Madison and Milwaukee are nothing like Chicago or New York, but I thought that my bigger worldview would somehow be helpful when introducing the proverbial country mouse to the city. Man, was I wrong."

Both of his friends jumped in before Brady deferred to Penny. "Don't tell me that you actually thought you needed to protect your mom from the big city? She's the fiercest woman I know."

"No. I always knew she was strong. I just thought she might be anxious traveling to the city. Other than occasional trips to her sister's in suburban Minneapolis, we've never traveled to a city together."

Now it was Brady's turn to jump in. "So, you thought she'd cower at the sight of a building taller than a grain elevator? What else do you think us bumpkins are scared of?"

"Clearly I'm not explaining this very well." Joshua again tried to share his revelations about his mother. He had no intention of suggesting that she needed him as a protector. Nor did he harbor any elitist views concerning those who choose to live in small towns.

"Relax. We're just bustin' your chops. And you deserve it. As smart as you are you're still as thick as a pregnant sow."

"I don't know jack about pig farming, but Brady's right. There's a reason we chose her as our second mom. She never judged me, but never let me off the hook either. I remember the day I came home from high school with a note for my mom to call the principal. That was the day I asked Ms. Jenkins if she knew what they called a female dog, because she sure was acting like one. I thought I had walked right up to the line of what I could get away with. Turns out I was wrong. My mom was furious, and she told my dad that he, too, should be furious. I told her I was sorry, and she yelled at me, 'Well, Penelope, you can't unscramble eggs! You're grounded.'

"Later that week I got a temporary reprieve because my folks were out of town. The only place they'd let me go was the diner. I was struggling with the apology letter when your mom checked in on me. I told her what my mom had said. She paused, gave it some thought, and said, 'Your mom's right. If we can't unscramble the eggs, what can we do with them?' She had me write an entire list of all the things we could make with eggs: breakfast burritos, quiche Lorraine, French toast, all sorts of breads, huevos rancheros, and on and on. After we looked at the list, she had me read it back to her. 'Hmmm, I see. So, what do you want to make? I think something sweet might taste nice.'

"Then she told me to put on my coat and she walked me over to Kieffer's Drug Store. We picked out a stuffed puppy, a gift bag, and a card, and we wrote the following note:

"'Dear Ms. Jenkins, my name is Buffy the Bad Word Slayer. My friend Penelope is so sorry for being disrespectful with her actions

54

and her words. I told her that my friends and I also do not like that word. She told me that it won't happen again. Sincerely, Miss Buffy (but really Penelope).'"

Confused, Brady asked, "I understand the dog bit, but why did she make you write a list?"

"Look who's being thick now," Josh couldn't resist. "What was it, thicker than a pregnant sow?"

"Yeah, I thought that was a pretty good description of you. At least I didn't call you a little bi.."

That drew Penny into their budding verbal scrum. "Hey now. I never called her that. I said she was acting like one. And, to this day, when I do something awful I make a list of all the possible options in front of me. Your mom taught me that. No lesson plan. No syllabus. Just an exceptional outlook on life. Ms. Jenkins actually returned Buffy to me at graduation and I still have her in my apartment. Hands down the best lesson I've ever gotten on how to apologize. That's your mom."

Joshua knew that Penny was speaking the truth, for how many times had he been offered a twisted parable from his mom? In his mind he could rattle off several without missing a beat.

"Joshua, actions may speak louder than words, but loud isn't always necessary."

"Give a man a fish and feed him for a day. Teach a man to fish and feed him for a lifetime. Fry a man some fish and he'll come back every Friday night."

"Don't put all of your eggs in one basket may be sound advice from your financial advisor, but don't ever be afraid to bet everything on yourself."

"A leopard can't change its spots, but I tend to think that behaviors are more than skin deep."

He couldn't remember the circumstances for each of those comments, but he might have to consider writing some of them down. He'd never thought of how often she used such statements. Yet again, his mother was surprising him. Maybe his friends were right. Maybe he'd been too focused on himself to ever consider that his mother had her own life. Maybe thirty is when kids start to think differently about their parents. Maybe Brady was right. Maybe he was that thick. At any rate, he was here now. He was learning about his mom. He just hoped that he could use his knowledge and skills to help her navigate the lawsuit from Ted Wellington.

10—On the Origins of Ted Wellington

Ted Wellington had two sisters. Neither of them could recall him eating a jelly and peanut butter sandwich as a child. They agreed with Ted that it probably happened, they just couldn't remember it. Most meals came to them by way of the live-in help, Maria, a young Australian woman who may have overstayed her visa. On the rare occasion that their mother prepared a meal, it was most often something that required no cooking and minimal preparation. A jelly and peanut butter sandwich certainly met the criteria. Ted's father was an attorney who worked in mergers and acquisitions. He worked too hard, slept too little, and enjoyed the city social scene too much.

Spending his childhood years in suburban Houston, Ted ventured as far as SMU to pursue a degree in finance. He followed that up by investing three years in an Ivy League law degree. At twenty-five, he tired of following his father's prescribed program. He had no desire to end up in politics, and did not envision a future that led to being a governor or senator. In a prior generation, his conviction on charges of sexual misconduct during his junior year in Dallas would've been disqualifying. America was either becoming more forgiving or more apathetic toward the indiscretions of their politicians. Regardless, he removed himself from that arena, viewing the role of politician as too restrictive. Ribbon-cutting ceremonies and riding in parades held no interest for him. Ted's true passion, and his greatest skill, was making money. Eschewing fundraising galas in favor of wooing investors, Ted took the $10 million he received from his parents and grew it to over $2 billion.

After the first billion he turned much of the day-to-day business over to other team members. In its early years, Three Corners, LLC, didn't make or build anything. Rather, they purchased existing businesses and helped them become better at generating revenue. There was nothing magic to it, just an extremely focused approach to making money. Ted was always amazed at how many great business minds lost sight of revenue generation when developing and analyzing advanced metrics. Now that his stake in the company was over $2 billion, Ted devoted his time to other projects. Massive battery storage for solar arrays, wind turbines, electrical grids, and data centers were all hobbies of his. He even joined the board of directors of a small nonprofit working in cancer research. The inefficiency of scientific research bothered him. He couldn't reconcile the time-consuming regulations when people's lives were at stake. He was a bull in the proverbial china shop on the board, but he kept with it. When people asked about his interest in serving on the board, he told a vague story of Maria, his childhood nanny who left her role when she was diagnosed with renal cancer. The greater truth was that Ted wanted to see just how much it would cost to cure cancer. And then, on the back end, how much money could be made from a life-saving treatment.

Ted's other pet project at the moment was trying to own the newly famous jelly and peanut butter sandwich. Like many narcissists, Ted knew that he was special and deserved his place in history. Elvis had his peanut butter, banana, and bacon sandwich. Arnold Palmer had iced tea and lemonade. Ted Wellington wanted to be remembered for his genius as well as his wealth. In his mind there were plenty of quirky capitalists throughout American history. He needed to showcase that he was more than rich. He was also brilliant—for who else would think to pair jelly and peanut butter to create a new sandwich? Some billionaires added to their renown through fashion, wearing the same hoodie sweatshirt all the time. Others chose odd hobbies, like collecting Komodo dragons. Still others stuck to the cheap look of a bowl haircut. None of these appealed to Ted. He would be remembered for having created something. And, in the absence of any good ideas of his own, he took aim at the newly crowned sandwich of the year.

Too much attention had been paid to this Betty Einfach from Wisconsin. In her own words, she hadn't created anything that someone else couldn't have done. It was simple. It was brilliant. It would be enduring. This was how Ted wanted to be remembered. The only problem standing in his way was a simpleton from a forgettable small town.

Winning his trademark case was one thing; he needed for Betty to go away. So, Ted took matters into his own hands and hired a private investigator to learn more about this woman from El Grain, Wisconsin. After a mere four days, the PI excitedly called Ted.

"First off, before I share my findings, I want to be assured that you'll pay me for the full two-month contract you signed. Just because I work fast doesn't mean that I shouldn't get paid."

"Assuming what you have is worthwhile, then certainly I will honor your contract."

"Good. You need to come to town. I've arranged for a second interview with some townsfolk. I want you to hear what they have to say. It appears that Miss Betty may not be as wholesome as the media would have you believe."

"You better not be wasting my time."

"I'm not. Just be here on Sunday. You'll want to give me a bonus."

"We'll see about that."

+ + + + +

"Mom, I know you don't care about the name of your sandwich, but I'm afraid this guy is going to bankrupt you with court filings that require a response. I'm not well-versed in this area of law. I don't know how much I can help. I think we've got to find a way to make it go away."

"I understand, but I'm not worried."

"Do you really understand what I'm talking about?"

"Of course I do, Joshua. Do you remember my friend Carl Maier? He's a Certified Master Cheese Maker, but even so, his degree is in Colby. He once told me there are over six hundred different types of cheese made in Wisconsin. Carl's a great cheese maker, but he's only a master of one. And, if I'm being honest, I don't think his Colby is the best one he makes. You see, I don't need you to be a master of trademark law, you're a good lawyer and plenty smart enough to figure this out. Also, I'm not going to waste my time worrying about the name of a sandwich."

"Ah, yes, the famous making cheese is like being a lawyer analogy." He was a bit annoyed by his mother's complacency on this matter. "Can you at least show a little concern? You'll be happy to know that I remember a little bit from you dragging me to church. Doesn't the Bible verse say, 'Money is the root of all evil'? This guy Ted, he has money, he knows how to make money, and for whatever stupid reason he has his sights on you."

She mildly corrected him. "They do say that money is the root of all kinds of evil. And if that's true, perhaps inherited wealth is the fruit of that tree. But what does it say about this man that he is willing to spend money, time, and energy on a fight over a sandwich? Whose attention or love is he so desperately seeking? I don't think I need to be afraid of him. No. Something's got him bound. I think I feel sorry for him."

11 – On Sandwiches as a Trail Snack

Kristin Jorgensen was the semi-retired pastor who Betty Einfach considered her oldest friend in all of El Grain. Truth is, the feeling was mutual. Pastor Kristin had a wonderfully large, loving family, but strangely enough she did not have too many girlfriends in town. Even with a good decade between them, their friendship came easily. Betty had looked to Pastor Kristin for advice on several occasions, more so as a friend than her spiritual shepherd. Likewise, Kristin enjoyed Betty's kinship precisely because she wasn't a parishioner. There was a period during Joshua's school years that Betty took him to church. She liked listening to Kristin preach, but church membership never resonated with her. She liked to think of herself as a believer, but she swore that the lights dimmed just a little bit every time she stepped foot in the sanctuary. Pastor Kristin walked her through confession and forgiveness, assuring her that God was not the source of the judgment she was feeling—nor were the lights dimming at her mere presence. She asked Betty once if she was judging herself. She wasn't. The judgment she felt was emanating from the people in the pews. She preferred to worship God outside of the organized Church. And while that is a crutch used by many to avoid church altogether, Betty meant it, and Kristin believed her.

In the fall of 2010, when Joshua was fifteen, one of his classmates was in a head-on collision with a married mother of two. Both were killed instantly. Max, the teenager, had traces of alcohol in his system. Norene Wofford, the mother, did not. Yet she was the driver who swerved into Max's lane. It was a terrible tragedy for the entire town of El Grain. Max was a member of Kristin's church, and she needed to find the words to speak at his funeral. Some people in town urged her to preach on the dangers of drunk driving. Many others wanted her to publicly criticize the distracted driver for taking the life of a young Christian man. Still others called in to offer their thoughts and prayers while also hoping to suss out any gossipy details that Pastor Kristin might share. It was one of the saddest moments of Pastor Kristin's career. She had baptized and confirmed Max, and now she was going to bury him.

Amidst that noise, she remembered something. It was a short handwritten note from Betty that read, "I've concluded I am not wise enough to make sense of this tragedy. I shall no longer attempt to do so. I am grateful for you, for I know your words shall be enough." That message got Kristin through Max's funeral, and soon after that, Kristin and Betty started taking regular trips out to Kugel's Springs to go for a walk in the woods.

When Betty pulled up, the nearly seventy-year-old pastor was already busy stretching out. After greetings and some small talk they were ready to tackle their usual loop. They liked it because it gave them plenty of time to catch up, but not so long that they needed to make a full day of it.

"So, where are you helping out these days?"

"Oh, the bishop asked me to take an interim call over in Eau Claire. Their pastor moved to Iowa. They think it'll take four to six months to replace him. Mostly they just want me to preach on Sundays. It's a hike, but I'll take it if they want me."

"What do you mean 'if they want' you? They're the ones needing a pastor."

"Well, I may have disinvited myself."

"How so?"

During the meet-and-greet with the church council, Pastor Kristin pulled no punches. A man her age asked a pretty pointed question about whether she was one of those pastors who put their pronouns on their name tag. She knew what the man wanted to hear. She refused to play along. Instead of providing additional comfort to a man who already looked comfortable, she needled him just enough to make him squirm.

"I turned to the man and assured him that throughout my career I've been known as a woman. However, when it comes to the Holy Trinity, I do refer to God as they/them. He got pretty red in the face, which is when I dialed it back just a bit. But I don't imagine I'll get an invitation to serve as their interim. How about you? Tell me about this sandwich craze!"

By the tone of her texts, Kristin knew that Betty wanted to talk about the fact that she'd been in the news lately. And, while Betty had been OK with the idea of going to Nashville and Los Angeles, she generally stayed away from too much publicity in her own town. Of course, Kristin knew all about why she was reticent to step back into the limelight, and was happy for the chance to talk with her friend.

"It's been great having Joshua around. I don't pretend to think that he'll move back to El Grain on a permanent basis, but I'll enjoy it while it lasts."

"How's he keeping himself busy?"

"His firm is letting him run his business from up here. And, he's picked up a few local clients as I understand it. But if you ask me, I think he's spending all his time on this lawsuit that was filed against me."

"You mentioned that. What's the issue with your sandwich?"

"As Joshua tells me, it's not so much about the sandwich as what it's called. Apparently, you can trademark a name like 'jelly and peanut butter sandwich' but not the sandwich itself. So, I'm free to sell the sandwiches, I just can't use the name."

"So, you're telling me I could trademark something like St. John's Lutheran Church and no one else could use it?"

"I don't think it's that easy. Remember when you tried to use a punny name for the canned soup drive in January and got a letter from the NFL to cease and desist, so you changed the spelling to The Souper Bowl of Caring? I think it's more like that. Right now, Joshua is in court arguing that I should be able to use 'jelly with peanut butter sandwich.' We'll see how it goes."

"How can you trademark that? Everyone has jelly and peanut butter in their pantry. I'm sorry you're caught in the middle of all this."

"Apparently trademark protection exists to help protect a business's reputation. This Ted Wellington wants there to be no confusion that he invented jelly and peanut butter sandwiches. Trademarking the name will help him protect his reputation and avoid confusion for who ought to benefit, and allow him to receive compensation from the sandwich's name. He claims he created the sandwich as a child and didn't need to trademark it until he saw my version. He says he only filed the trademark to protect his interests."

"Do you think any of that's true?"

"I know for a fact that it's not true, but none of that really matters. It's just a sandwich. Joshua thinks that winning that Sammie Award really helps make the case that I created the sandwich. He also said that's why Ted was so insistent on interrupting my speech to plant some doubt about its origin. Honestly, can you think of anything more ridiculous than fighting over the history of a common sandwich?"

"Is there really much money to be made off of this sandwich? I guess I don't see it, but I'm a pastor and not an MBA."

"Joshua keeps telling me to 'go big or go home.' He's convinced that the success of this sandwich will help me retire. I asked him, 'Why do I have to go anywhere? I'm already at home.'"

"I would've been terrible in business. He must see something that I just don't get."

"Well, you can check it out for yourself. I brought a few with me for our mid-hike snack. It's kind of where they do their best work—feeding hungry people."

In typical fashion, during the first half of their hike Betty and Kristin caught up on each other's lives. During the second half, Kristin always liked to ask questions. Today's question had to do with her husband's desire to go see the B-52s in Las Vegas.

"I don't see the appeal. The members have got to be my age or older. He says it's on his bucket list. We'll probably go, but I'll definitely be leaving my hearing aids in the hotel room. My question for you today is this: What is the most memorable concert you have attended?"

"I know exactly how I'm going to answer this one. It's actually been on my mind a lot lately."

+ + + + +

In the summer of 1992 Betty Einfach was between jobs. She was young and a bit directionless. On a whim, she called up a childhood friend. Emily was heading down to Chicago to attend something called the Lollapalooza festival with her boyfriend. She promised a great day of music with Pearl Jam, Soundgarden, Red Hot Chili Peppers, and a ton of other bands. Having no other plans, Betty jumped on the idea. She didn't even mind being the third wheel. The festival was amazing, but the real fun was the activity happening outside of the World Music Theater.

The venue had only been around for a couple of years, a fact that was quite obvious from the surroundings. As it was built on a wide-open acreage of flat land, the designers had to manufacture a hillside so they could have amphitheater-like lawn seating. The fake hill surrounded by flatness on all sides had all the beauty of modern suburban design. The parking lot wasn't any better. The golf ball–sized gravel had been rolled flat, but it still wasn't the appropriate size for a gravel driveway. There were no markers indicating where people should park. Instead the park relied on a high school–aged workforce to create some semblance of straight lines for parking. With such minimal effort put into the security and parking lot, it made for a lawless, Wild West atmosphere. Certainly a place where one could have some fun, but also where some terrible things could happen.

Having lost her friends, Betty found herself wandering the parking lot. There she came across a young woman being harassed by two men. Judging by what they were asking, Betty easily figured out that this woman wanted nothing to do with the men. Instinctively, she yelled out for the woman, "Charlotte, is that you? I've been looking all over for you. Brett and Marcus are waiting for us. Let's go." All of this she spoke loudly for others to hear as she approached the unknown woman and escorted her away from who knows what was about to happen.

"Come on, Char. Let's go."

"Thank you…"

"Betty. I'm Betty," she whispered.

"Hi. I'm M…"

"No. For the moment, you're Char."

The two women walked with a purpose until they felt comfortable among a crowd of other people. Having lost both the creeps in the parking lot and the friends they came with, the two women walked around the festival for a few hours together. Charlotte was high as a kite. Betty didn't feel comfortable leaving her alone. Eventually they caught up with Emily and Bart and the four of them enjoyed the inimitable voice of Chris Cornell and Soundgarden. At the end of the evening, Char and Betty exchanged phone numbers, once Char had safely located her friends.

+ + + + +

"Now that sounds adventurous. Much more so than listening to Love Shack sponsored by AARP."

"The B-52s are great. Why are you complaining about them?"

"I'm sure they're fine, I just feel like my concert days are behind me."

"Well, mine weren't, because that first Lollapalooza story was just half of my answer. A couple of weeks later I got a phone call."

+ + + + +

"Betty, this is Maria."

"Maria?"

"Sorry, this is Char from Lollapalooza."

"Holy cow. Char, it's good to hear from you."

"I wanted to thank you for helping me out back in Chicago. How would you like to go to another Lollapalooza show?"

"Really? You want to go through that again?"

"Yeah. The tour is coming through Texas in a few weeks. This one's all on me. I've got a cush job, a place to stay, and plenty of food. All you've got to do is get yourself down here. I'll take care of the rest. And I'll stay sober this time so you don't have to rescue me."

"That sounds amazing. Count me in."

Once she got to Texas, Charlotte-Maria had truly taken care of the rest. The details initially seemed a little sketchy, but Maria had access to a poolside apartment at an enormous estate in a gated community. After getting settled and taking a dip in the pool, Maria told Betty about the plans for the concert. She had failed to tell Betty that the reason there was an extra ticket was because of a recent breakup. Maria was seeing a guy she called Jimbo. He had a brother, Randy, who had recently been dumped by Rachel. Betty was Rachel's replacement. A fact that might have been nice to know ahead of time.

+ + + + +

"So, there I am, a young single woman from Minnesota, getting ready for an eight-hour blind date at Lollapalooza with a tobacco-chewing guy named Randy from Seguin. All because I helped a girl escape two creepy guys a few weeks earlier."

"You've lived many lives, Betty. So, how did it go?"

"It actually went really well even though Charlotte-Maria lied about staying sober. Randy was a gentleman about the whole thing. Mostly he talked about Rachel. The breakup was clearly one-sided. It got momentarily weird when he tried to kiss me while he still had chewing tobacco in his mouth. Did you know that tobacco could have a wintergreen flavor?"

"No. Betty, you didn't?"

"I'm kidding. I told him he should try and win back Rachel. They dropped us off at the mansion around midnight and I tucked a drunken Charlotte-Maria into bed. I heard from him a few years later. Rachel never did take him back."

Of course there was much more to share, but judging by Kristin's concerned look she decided to stop there for the day.

Besides, they were already back at the trailhead, having completed the four-mile loop.

12—On Celebrity Branding

While the American public was enjoying the latest trend in sandwiches, celebrity business managers were ready to capitalize on a money-making opportunity. For decades athletes endorsed shoes and clothing brands at a national level. Meanwhile, on a more local level they would endorse car dealerships, restaurants, and grocery stores. Athletic careers are notoriously short, so agents were willing to jump at almost any chance to supplement their athletes' income while they were still on their respective rosters.

Of course, transcendent athletes could lengthen their time in the sun by branding their own shoe line. Well-spoken athletes could parlay their success on the field into a broadcast booth. Opinionated stars could find work as a pundit on television, radio, or podcasts. Charismatic athletes often left sports altogether, in hopes of finding success as an actor or politician. All of these viable options for a post-playing career had been around for ages.

Only more recently could the high-achieving, well-spoken, good-looking athlete, with the right coaching, become themselves a brand. People would pay to emulate their favorite athletes. What does Serena Williams eat? What is Tom Brady's workout routine? What podcasts does Caitlin Clark follow? Where does LeBron James vacation? These athletes, with their appeal, were big business. Their face and body were the public image of the business, but their million-dollar payrolls showcased just how many people they employed to keep the business moving forward.

Jackson Bryant was the first agent to seize on the jelly and peanut butter opportunity. Truthfully, he wasn't much of an agent. He signed on to help a childhood friend while he studied for professional exams. The future actuary's one and only client was Joe Thompson. The massive left tackle was a consensus first-round pick in the upcoming NFL draft. At six-foot-four and 320 pounds, the farm kid from western Iowa finished college having given up one sack in four years as the starting left tackle. He was everything that was right with college athletics at a time when nearly everything else was wrong.

J.T., as he was known by friends, grew up on a hog farm outside of Sioux City, Iowa, where he earned all-state honors for both football and track and field. When he wasn't on the field, he earned his Eagle Scout rank and was inducted into the National Honor Society during his junior year. He committed to the University of Iowa without any fanfare. An intern from ESPNU showed up at his house on signing day to ask him about his plans for college because at the time he maintained no social media presence. Reportedly, he took a break from chores for all of three seconds to point to the Hawkeye on his hat.

While at Iowa, he studied political science with a particular interest in agriculture policy. As a kid he watched his family take on more and more hogs to keep the farm afloat. His parents didn't like it and felt that larger farms would ultimately push out family farms altogether, with little regard for the detrimental impact of too many hogs in a concentrated area. His dad always said, "Dilution is the solution to pollution." It was an issue that Joe planned to pursue after college. He would give the NFL a few years, but only enough to build sufficient cash reserves and recognition to freely pursue this core purpose. Focusing on his academic degree precluded J.T. from ever considering the transfer portal, even as the Hawkeyes struggled through a four-win season. His loyalty to his state university was about to pay off in a major way.

J.B. and J.T. were the closest of friends in elementary school until Jackson and his family moved to Missouri during middle school. The boys kept in touch online through Minecraft for years to come. J.B. was never an athlete, but he and J.T. shared a similar level of commitment to their pursuits. To support his friend, J.B. built a replica of Kinnick Stadium in their Minecraft world. He even added the local children's hospital across the street that became famous in 2017 when fans started waving to the children in the hospital after the first quarter of every home game. This friendship forged in farm fields and maintained in Minecraft was about to enter a new phase. On the verge of NFL stardom, Joe Thompson was also set to become the first athlete to make his own line of peanut butter.

Pancake brand peanut butter was a play on the fact that Joe Thompson was known for his flattening pancake blocks on running plays. J.B. couldn't get approval to use the Hawkeye logo in the branding, but that was OK. He didn't want to be married to any one image before Joe got selected in the draft. He settled on generic colors and a marketing plan that included J.T.'s Pancake Peanut Butter, "It's not just for pancakes." He worked with Joe to create online workout videos demonstrating Joe's incredible strength, while taking a break between sets to dig his spoon into a jar of his own peanut butter. J.B. made sure that every pre-draft interview had a jar of peanut butter in the background and his plan was working. The website was inundated with requests for where to buy J.T.'s Pancake Peanut Butter. Depending on where Joe was selected in the draft, J.B. was working on where to sign distribution agreements. It was such a natural fit for a strong, up-and-coming athlete to tout protein-packed peanut butter. J.T.'s Pancake Peanut Butter was projected to become the fourth biggest peanut butter company in the states. J.T. and J.B. had no intention of creating the Joe Thompson Lifestyle Company, but it's unwise to step in front of a boulder's path when it's coming down the mountain—even for the best pass-blocking tackle of the twenty-first century.

+ + + + +

Even more than peanut butter, jelly was having a true moment. Many celebrity business managers sniffed out the opportunity and were looking for the best place to strike. Having found success with fragrances and alcohols, they hoped to capitalize on this moment with vanity jams and jellies. One celebrity hoping to make a splash was April May, the thirty-year-old star looking for the next step in a transition from child star, to pop sensation and acclaimed actor, into the world of lifestyle maven. Following the successful launch of her Spring Botanicals line of teas and fragrances, April May was in the midst of rebranding to Spring+ on the advice of her chief marketing officer, who was also her sister.

Market research led the team to believe that preserves sounded better than jelly for their brand appeal. Citing the source of their berries was also important. When Spring+ was ready to launch, this research became useful as they launched Spring+ Maine Blueberry Preserves, Georgia Peach Preserves, and Washington Raspberry Preserves.

April didn't have the same catalog of songs and films as other more famous teen sensations. The confusion between Spring Botanicals and Spring+ also made it difficult for fans to connect these dots to April May. They had good counsel around them, but April and her sister, Pam, were just so insistent on managing all the details that they couldn't break through to the national scene. So, worried about the backlash from too much exposure, April May and her Spring+ line of products was not on track to achieve much market penetration in the crowded space of celebrity jams and jellies.

+ + + + +

"Why do you suppose an Oscar-winning actor needs his own line of vodka?" Penny asked idly as she and Josh watched the pre-game warm-ups on the ice. She continued, without waiting for an answer, "Our firm still uses celebrities to endorse products in our ads, but it seems like they all want their own product line these days. Or at least their agents do. We've been working on a local car campaign and were in negotiations with the third baseman for the Twins, Sam Arias. It's a simple eight-second sound bite. We're all set for the shoot and his agent says he wants a stake in the dealership. I told the guy it's a small campaign that'll air on cable television for six weeks, hardly worth a stake in the company. They walked away. The owner of the dealership got his nephew to read the lines and we moved on."

"I've always liked Arias. Local kid makes good. He doesn't come across so uppity."

"He's got an agent in his ear about free agency, looking for a bigger market, that kind of stuff... What do you think of these seats?"

"They're nice. How often do you get to use them?"

The marketing and advertising agency where Penny worked had a suite for the Minnesota Wild games. Often used for wooing clients, there were no VIPs in town for today's game, so the firm made the seats available to their own staff. Penny was an account executive at the firm. Joshua didn't know exactly what that encompassed, but he knew it involved sales and that she was doing quite well. It was a last-minute invitation to attend tonight's game with her, but they were both glad for the chance to visit. It was a long enough drive that Joshua planned to make a night of it and crash at Penny's place as she had a condo across the river in Minneapolis.

They enjoyed the first two periods with about a dozen other colleagues and their guests. And, since the tickets were free, many of those guests left by the start of the third period. The game was tied, but that wasn't enough to keep casual fans out too late on a weeknight. Joshua and Penny intended to stay through the conclusion. Joshua had updated her on all the details of his mother's lawsuit and he heard plenty about Penny's clients.

"Maybe your mom needs a celebrity endorsement."

"How would that help?"

"If the public knows more about your mom, and she has public sentiment on her side, it won't matter what any courtroom has to say. Better products don't always win, better marketing does."

"I doubt that my mom would be interested in a celebrity campaign, but I do like the idea of winning in the court of public opinion."

13—On Feeding Hungry People

"Betty, thanks for joining me today. I couldn't help but ask you to join me after your comment about feeding hungry people last week."

"Of course. Your invitation was just the push I needed."

The soup kitchen at Our Savior's Lutheran Church was a weekly community meal hosted by retired members of the church. It was an open meal to all community members, but the mission was to provide a meal over the lunch hour every Wednesday for anyone in need. Partnering with St. Bernard's Catholic Church, Wisconsin Avenue Methodist Church, and the El Grain Community Church, hungry community members could find a place to eat on Monday through Thursday from September through May. The churches never intended to be the singular solution for all food insecurity in town, but churches could do worse than following Jesus's command to feed the hungry.

Each church did things a bit differently, but they all committed to providing a hot meal between 11 a.m. and 1 p.m. from Labor Day through Memorial Day. The schedule not only provided routine for those in need, but it also helped local social service workers know where to show up, for hunger is often accompanied by other issues like homelessness or behavioral and physical health concerns.

St. Bernard's was famous for hearty soups and gracious amounts of bread. The Methodists always provided a variety of foods, potluck style. The community church had a faithful team of cooks who prepared several trays of casseroles, ensuring plenty of carbs, vegetables, and protein. The Lutherans were best known for their desserts. You were guaranteed plenty of butter, sugar, and hot coffee at Our Savior's. The desserts also made for good takeaway food at the end of your meal.

Pastor Kristin was always looking for something that guests could take with them on their way out the door. Snacks for later. Other than desserts, she would sometimes corral enough apples, bananas, or oranges to pass along. Other times it was bags of chips, nuts, or granola. Her hike with Betty had given her an idea and Betty was more than willing to help out. Toting a box with fifty jelly and peanut butter sandwiches, this would be ideal sustenance for later.

"You'll stick around to eat with us?"

"Yes. Put me to work. I've got Hazel minding the diner for the next couple of hours. She was nervous, but she'll be fine. Where do we get started?"

Heading into the kitchen, Kristin introduced Betty to Carl, Bob, Connie, Ginnie, Linda, and Walt. A good group of volunteers for the couple of dozen guests they were expecting. Betty and Bob ended up on dishes and cleanup, but not before Connie warned her to ignore any of Bob's ridiculous stories and jokes. He was an aspiring grandpa, having recently retired from teaching social studies.

"Bob, I've got to be honest, you look really young to be retired."

"I'm fifty-seven, but I put in thirty-five years with tweens and teens at the middle school. Raised and launched three of our own. Now I get to be selfish."

"Selfish, eh? Like serving meals at a soup kitchen? I'm guessing you've got work to do if you're trying to be selfish."

"Well, let me tell you, I did head into the Cities for a concert recently."

From across the room, Connie jumped in. "Don't tell that dumb concert story. We want Betty to come back and help us again sometime."

"It's a good story."

"Sure. Twenty years ago. For your middle schoolers."

Enjoying the dynamic, Betty chimed in, "I thought you said this was a recent concert."

"It was a recent concert, and if Connie will stick to her own duties and mind her own business, I'll tell you about it."

"Whatever," he could hear his wife respond while tending to the food in the commercial oven.

"As I was saying, there's an artist in town, Alex Dimitros. Greek guy, excellent potter. Vases, platters, mugs, you name it, he makes it."

"Can't say I know the name."

"That's OK. At any rate, it turns out he's something of a renaissance man. Besides his tremendous pottery, he's a nationally renowned violinist. Keeps that stuff to himself. He's the quietest Greek guy I've ever met.

"A couple of weeks ago, the Wet Bandits were scheduled to come to Minneapolis for a show. We'd never seen them in person, but I'd really wanted to."

"Again, I've never heard of them." Betty didn't even know that she was playing her part perfectly for Bob's story.

"That's OK. They're a wonderful choir and it's kind of a clever name. They're a group of former prisoners from Seattle. Having all served their time, they chose Wet Bandits as an homage to the movie *Home Alone*. It rains a lot in Seattle and they were all criminals. A bit of a pun. Kind of clever. And if that wasn't enough, instead of choir robes, they all wear these trench coats as their uniform. You know, like a gabardine rainproof type fabric.

"So, it turns out their soloist got sick at the last minute and couldn't make the trip. They arrived in Minneapolis with no violinist. They called around town, but the symphony orchestra is over in Finland. Then the director remembers a distant cousin who lives in Wisconsin and gives him a call. Alex takes the call and agrees to perform with the choir, so now the full concert is back on and they don't have to skip that piece of music.

"Meanwhile, Connie runs into Alex's yia yia at the grocery store. She's so proud that her grandson is going to be playing in the concert that she's giving out tickets to people she hardly even knows. Connie scoops up a pair for us as a retirement gift to me.

"We get to the concert. It turns out we're in the second row with all of Alex's family. I have no idea how, but his mother snuck in a whole plate of baklava. His thea had a tray of feta and olives. It was just a huge party atmosphere that we got to be a part of. When it's his time to come on stage, instead of wearing a trench coat like the choir, he's wearing a short-sleeved polo with the blue and white design of the Greek flag. His family is clapping and cheering and all I can think is how this man's arms have got to be the hairiest arms I've ever seen. How does he possibly do pottery? The clay has got to be a pain to clean off of his hirsute arms.

"Then he played the concert. It was alright."

Unknowingly having taken the bait, Betty jumped in. "It was just alright? All that build-up and no details about the actual performance?"

"I mean I guess I could share more about the music. I was just excited that I got to see hairy potter and the gabardine choir."

Unsure how to react, Betty paused for a beat. Connie walked over and put her arm around her. "Yeah, thirty-five years with this guy."

"Do you get it? Gabardine choir; goblet of fire. That's good stuff."

"No, I get it. And I do appreciate the commitment. That's a really long walk to get to that punchline. I am curious though; how did it land with your students? Like, do today's kids even know what gabardine is?"

Bob was more than willing to let the ladies roll their eyes and make fun of him. Having spent a career in middle school, he was used to it. Betty and Connie were right though, that story was now twenty years old. He'd need to write some new material in retirement. He also needed one of his kids to get married and have kids. Grandkids were a great audience.

"What if I made up a story about a sorcerer's clone? I mean I'd love to replace Azkaban, but I've never found a word that fits."

"Bob, using a different book won't make it any funnier. You need to just give up on your Greek hairy potter. Let's not scare away new volunteers with your dated malapropisms."

Bob also knew that his willingness to play the fool was disarming. He was a young teacher when Betty moved to town. She didn't know him, but he knew of her. He also knew that this town hadn't always been kind to her—some of it was her own doing. He didn't know if she had any reservations about coming to help out at the soup kitchen, but he always wanted to make people feel welcome. For you never know when someone is going to need a friend.

14—On the Rise and Fall of Trends

While Betty continued to use her same basic recipe for a jelly and peanut butter sandwich while feeding the hungry, restaurants around the country were exploring with this new pairing as evidenced by the following menu write-ups and accompanying reviews from famed food critic Johann Volkers.

Enoki, Napa Valley – Our deconstructed jelly and peanut butter sandwich features several slices of sourdough crostini, a generous portion of our house-made creamy almond butter, and organic small batch strawberry preserves from the award-winning Valenti Family Farm.

"Enoki is one of my favorite restaurants to visit when in Napa, so I was truly excited to try their version of a jelly and peanut butter sandwich. I found no fun or whimsy in their offering. It is clearly an afterthought on their otherwise well-balanced menu. I can just as easily plop a scoop of peanut butter and jelly onto a plate at home. The individual elements save this sandwich, as they are all grown and produced locally. I'd recommend the beet salad before ordering this again, and you all know how much I loathe beets."

Tiina's Deli, Ishpeming, Michigan – The Finnish restaurateur didn't bother to reprint her menu, but I did find the following on her "Specials" board. "Since everyone is asking, yes, I'll make you a sandwich of jelly and peanut butter using chunky peanut butter and lingonberry jam on whole wheat bread."

"While Tiina may confusingly spell her name with two i's, there is nothing confusing about this straightforward version of America's newest sandwich sensation. No pretense, no fuss, this uncomplicated version is exactly what a jelly and peanut butter sandwich should be. Honestly, I was only in the Upper Peninsula for a family funeral, so this was a pleasant surprise."

Jermaine's, Charlotte, North Carolina – Forget what you thought you knew about peanut butter and prepare yourself for the decadence of cashew butter. This nut butter pairs well with our chunky peach preserves from across the border in Georgia.

"I may not have forgotten everything I knew about peanut butter, but I did enjoy Jermaine's cashew butter. I've never been a fan of peach jam, but it's a solid entry and honestly I think I'm getting ready to eat something other than jelly and peanut butter."

Grace Land Café, Memphis, Tennessee – Had Elvis known, we're convinced that he would've added jelly to his peanut butter, banana, and bacon sandwich. Grape jelly completes this sandwich worthy of the King.

"No. This sandwich is nowhere near worthy of The King, A King, Larry King, or Don King. There are too many tastes going on in this sandwich. This is a great example of when a sandwich becomes less than the sum of its parts. This phenomenon needs to end. I've eaten a jelly and peanut butter sandwich for ninety-eight straight days. Make it stop."

Crustless, Your Local Grocer, Anywhere, USA – Now available in the frozen food aisle of your local grocery store, crustless jelly and peanut butter sandwiches. The package contains six grape jelly and six strawberry sandwiches. Simply take it out of the freezer and put it in your child's lunch. It'll be perfectly thawed by lunchtime.

"Absolutely not. Day 100 of consecutive jelly and peanut butter sandwiches will be my last. When I went to my grocery club warehouse I saw these in the freezer aisle and had to give it a try. It's true that they don't need a lot of time to thaw, but America, how long does it take to put jelly and peanut butter onto two slices of bread when making a school lunch? Somehow in the short time that jelly and peanut butter sandwiches have been a part of the zeitgeist of American

culture a company has already brought to market a more convenient version of the most convenient sandwich ever created. Let's take a look at our priorities. America has 26 million people without healthcare, there are wars being waged on three different continents, and Florida is on its way to being submerged by rising waters. In the pantheon of big problems, I can't imagine there was huge urgency behind getting quicker access to a jelly and peanut butter sandwich. Stop it! Stop it! Stop it! No more jelly and peanut butter!"

In retrospect, it may have been that last review that broke the jelly and peanut butter fever. Meanwhile, Johann Volkers wasn't the only one who noticed the proliferation of jelly and peanut butter sandwiches. Ted Wellington and his lawyers continued to monitor the situation. And, while they occasionally issued new cease-and-desist letters, Ted's focus remained squarely fixed on a small diner in Wisconsin and its graciously gritty owner.

15—On the Verge of Cancellation

"What'll it be today, Mr. Sundquist?"

"You know what, Hazel, I think I'm going to take a break from the jelly with peanut butter sandwich. I'd like to go with the meatloaf and a side salad."

"And to drink?"

"Coffee."

The Sunday crowd shuffled in, and for the first time in ages it seemed somewhat normal. There were a few orders for the jelly with peanut butter sandwich, but mostly people had returned to their old standbys. Being a Sunday, that meant anything from waffles to pot roast. Just one table over from Glenn Sundquist sat a visitor that no one recognized. Ted Wellington expected that he'd be spotted soon enough, but for now he was just gazing at the menu and wondering how anyone in their right mind would order coffee with their meatloaf. It wasn't the first thing in this town that he found odd.

Ted rolled into town the night before and lodged at the Sandhill Crane Bed and Breakfast. Ted's executive assistant, Tara Wilson, booked all of his travel. She was the only one he trusted to be mindful of his preferred amenities. Given the size of El Grain, he assumed she wouldn't be able to find a Conde Nast preferred location. At first glance, she seemed to have done well, but he ended up disappointed and poorly rested for his Sunday activities.

Staying in a room called The Chalet, he found the ski décor to be cluttered and noisy. What he found in the bathroom annoyed him even more. It's not that it was unclean, just not up to his standards. He made sure that the host knew about it when he went downstairs to grab a cup of coffee as they were preparing breakfast.

"I'd like to address the cleanliness of my room."

"Of course, sir. Was something not to your liking?"

"Well, you can take this as constructive criticism to better serve your customers in the future. The first time I used the toilet I noticed that it was almost out of toilet paper."

"Oh, I'm sorry, was there not another roll available?"

"There was, but when you leave an almost empty roll of toilet paper for a new customer, it gives the impression that the room has been previously used."

"I think that's a fair assumption."

"But a customer should never have to be thinking about that. Do you understand what I'm saying? Premier hotels always have a full roll on the dispenser when new guests arrive. And even then, they often make a nice triangular fold on the first square so that you know the bathroom has been well prepared before your arrival."

"But what do you do with all the half-rolls that go unused?"

"I don't know. Give them away to staff members. I don't care."

"I guess we could do that, but let me get the owners to help you out on this one."

"You can't make a decision about toilet paper?"

Ted really had a way of making people feel small.

After explaining his concerns to the owners, he was unsatisfied that he had been heard. The kind couple explained that it seemed wasteful and unnecessary to get rid of half-used rolls. They trusted their clients could put a new roll on the dispenser if needed. And, if not, they would be happy to send a well-trained staff member to do the job for him. Ted recognized the sarcasm in that last comment and decided it was not worth it to argue with this couple whose business would never amount to much with that attitude. When they asked him about joining them for breakfast he declined, packed up his bag, and walked out—telling them to bill his assistant.

That was the mood that followed Ted to his booth at Miss Betty's Diner, where he anxiously awaited Bert Corliss, the private investigator he had hired. Seeing him in the doorway, he curtly waved him over to the booth. They had agreed to meet at Miss Betty's Diner in order to prepare for their visits. It wasn't unusual for Ted to find himself in an unfamiliar town. He'd traveled extensively throughout his career. He was disappointed when he stepped into the diner. He wanted to hate it, but Betty kept things neat and tidy. The staff were pleasant and hospitable. The menus looked freshly printed touting a jelly with peanut butter sandwich, which was wrong, but allowable based on the current court instructions.

"So, you found the place alright?"

Ted brushed off the question by saying, "Just anxious to learn more about Miss Betty's history that has you so excited."

"Well, first of all, what would you say if I told you that she wasn't always known as Betty Einfach?"

"I'd say keep going."

"Excuse me. May I get you gentlemen anything to drink?"

Hazel's interruption aside, Bert and Ted shared a lengthy conversation about Betty and the town's history. Bert confessed that he only had one visit prepared for them, but the woman had pictures to accompany her story. He knew that Ted would be reluctant to come for just one visit, but Bert was certain that this interview would satisfy all of Ted's desires. He was willing to tell a little white lie given what he knew to be true. Upon leaving, they both felt satisfied with their meal and their plan. Ted had hoped to run into Betty at the diner, but he wasn't concerned—he would see her soon enough.

+ + + + +

Ted and Betty never crossed paths on Sunday afternoon because she was busy in the kitchen entertaining a guest from Chicago. At Betty's invitation, Big John Kowalczyk made the trek from Midlothian, Illinois, to El Grain for a weekend getaway. The two restaurateurs were busy sharing recipes and best practices for salvaging food that otherwise could easily go to waste. If it was a first date, it was surely an odd one. Honestly, neither of them knew what it was. They met at the Sammie Awards in Los Angeles and started texting after that. Mostly they texted back and forth about customers, servers, cooks, and food distributors. The tone changed when John asked about how her kid was doing.

Once they started talking about their kids, the texts got a bit longer and led to a few phone calls. John had two girls. They'd gone to live with their mother when she moved out and went back to Indiana. John made no apologies for who he was and the restaurant he ran. It's just that Deirdra expected a different lifestyle. When they divorced, she told John he could keep the restaurant, but she wanted the house. He obliged. She promptly sold the house and moved in with her folks in Merrillville. The restaurant had more equity, but she hadn't bothered to look into that. She worked as a dental hygienist and dreamed of the life that should have been hers. Unfortunately, while many good folk live in Midlothian and Merrillville, very few of them enjoy the standard of living that she felt she was owed. As for the girls, they loved their dad, even as their mom planted seeds about him being an underachiever. Thankfully, every time those seeds started to grow, they'd make a trip to dad's and remember how fun he was to be around. Well into adulthood, and after years of therapy, the girls started to realize that their dad was accomplishing all that he set out to achieve, it just wasn't what their mom wanted him to achieve. The divorce had been twenty years ago. Deirdra was remarried. Tricia, the eldest, was married with a son on the way. Julia was single, with a roommate, Drea. John had suspicions about the nature of their relationship, but he'd wait for Julia to bring it up on her own terms.

As these conversations progressed, it felt natural for Betty to invite John up to El Grain for a visit. John arrived late on Friday night and stayed in Betty's guest room. On Saturday, they went on a brewery tour at the One Good Eye Brewery before enjoying dinner with another couple. The foursome finished the night with some euchre back at Betty's place. On Sunday they spent all morning at the diner. When they closed after lunch, Betty promised John a walk through the downtown along the river before he needed to head back to Chicago.

"So, what'd you think of El Grain?"

"This has been fun. Can't tell you the last time I took a personal weekend. I do have a lingering question though."

Betty thought she knew where this was going, and she didn't know how to respond. What was this weekend? A date? They clearly enjoyed each other's company. They were unbothered by anything about each other's past. At the same time, it hadn't been romantic. Well, except for when John called her Costa Rican wildlife pictures erotic when he meant to say exotic. She didn't have a script. She'd simply go with whatever came out of her mouth.

"OK. Tell me about this lingering question."

"For the life of me, I can't figure out why they call it the One Good Eye Brewery. And no one would give a straight answer. Is this some sort of hazing for Chicagoans?"

That was not what she expected. And it didn't clear things up at all.

Getting no immediate response, he continued, "I guess I'll have to ask again next time I'm in town."

That was a little clearer.

+ + + + +

After their walk, John and Betty said their goodbyes. There was still a bit of light to the day, so Betty decided to continue her walk past the town hockey rinks. There were just two rinks assembled this year. The third location had been converted to a summer pickleball court and the pickleballers were adamant that flooding their court in the winter would cause cracks and leave the court uneven. Hockey and figure skaters were often at odds about ice time, but when it came to their disdain for pickleballers, their interests were aligned. *Screw you, boomer. Admit it, you're old. Leave our rinks alone.*

Late on Sunday afternoon the rink with boards was occupied by hockey players from age eight to sixty-eight. Men and women alike were skating, though all of the women were under thirty-five given the relative newness of competitive women's hockey. The second rink was full of free skaters of all levels. One pairs group was trying to show off with their throw double axel. Perhaps a bad choice given the congestion on the rink. Meanwhile, to help stay balanced, a young child was pushing a contraption made of PVC pipe with tennis balls attached to the bottom.

Betty spotted the Hartleys and headed their way. She wanted to let them know how much she appreciated Hazel's work at the diner. After sharing her gratitude, she couldn't help but notice a man on the far side of the hockey rink. He looked familiar, but in the fading light she wasn't certain who it was. Out of context, her mind didn't expect to see Ted Wellington in El Grain, so she hadn't even contemplated that it was him. He was standing next to another man and they started to walk her way. She wasn't worried as there were plenty of people around, but this didn't appear to be a friendly encounter. As they neared she heard his booming voice.

"Betty Einfach. Ted Wellington. I imagine you remember me."

"Of course," she yelled back. "What brings you to El Grain? If you're checking up on the diner, you'll be happy to know that we are following the court order and our menus only say that we offer jelly with peanut butter sandwiches."

"Yes, I was glad to see that when I ate there earlier today."

"Well, then, what can I do for you? I must say this is unexpected."

"Betty. You know what—I don't even think that's your real name."

"It is, Ted. Elizabeth Grace Einfach, and I go by Betty."

"Are you sure it's not Misty Meadows?" He said it loudly for everyone to hear.

Recognizing where this was going, she offered, "Ted, there are children around. Please. Let's go talk privately."

Her mind was racing. Was this intentional? How had he tracked her down? She didn't even know she'd be at the rink this evening. He must've been looking for a while if he'd already been to the restaurant. Calling her Misty Meadows could only mean one thing. She'd try once more to get him somewhere quieter.

"Ted, why don't we go back to the diner and have a visit. I'll make some food and we can talk about whatever you want."

"No. Everyone! Listen Up! Your dear beloved Miss Betty—the same woman who claims to have invented the jelly and peanut butter sandwich—used to go by the name Misty Meadows when she was a stripper."

Part Three

16—On the Encounter at Riverside Park

The rink where the free skaters roamed went quiet. Several stern looks were aimed in Ted's direction. Other faces shrugged, indicating that, *yeah, we knew that, we just don't talk about it.* Parents gathered their kids, unsure of what to make of the yelling man. Absorbed in the pickup game, skating continued on the hockey rink.

Ted wasn't convinced that this was the spectacle he was looking to create, but he was not the type to back down once committed. He wanted this news to become public, but judging by what he saw here he may have missed his mark. Betty held her hands up in a motion intended to bring calm. She was the one to break the silence.

"Ted, I see you've done some research."

The two looked each other over, each waiting for the other to speak. Meanwhile, a skater passed behind the far goal using the tight turn to slingshot himself forward as fast as his retired legs would allow. As Ted attempted to break the silence with another accusatory passage, in the corner of his eye he saw Bob Clark skating out of control in his direction. The man stumbled over the cap-rail of the two-foot-high boards of the hockey rink, crashing into Ted Wellington. He would go on to claim it was an accident, but it was the first time in twenty years of skating at the park that Bob had flown off the rink. Either way, it was enough of a distraction that people went back to their own business. Bob helped Ted to his feet, apologizing profusely for his poor skating.

"I guess that's why I was always a second-line skater on my high school team. I'm Bob Clark. Can I help you get cleaned off?"

"I'll be fine, thanks."

By this point, Betty had walked over and asked Ted for a chance to talk. He declined.

"I've said my piece. The truth about you will be told. I bet this new information will make a nice addition to our court filings."

"Filings?" the careless skater interrupted. "Yeah, I'm not so great at filing. I suppose if I'd done a better job on these blades I wouldn't have caught that edge and flown over the boards."

"Bob, is it? If you leave now, I might not sue you."

"You betcha. Again, my apologies."

Betty detected a smirk as Bob climbed back onto the ice, and a scowl from Ted as he departed the scene. Bob appeared to be pleased with himself. Ted's glare left no doubt that this matter was far from settled. As life returned to the skating rink, the Hartleys were the first to approach Betty.

"That was certainly interesting."

"Yes, he's the man who's suing me over the jelly and peanut butter sandwich. I imagine Hazel may have mentioned it. We're in court-ordered mediation right now."

"I see. So, this is about jealousy?"

"I'm not entirely sure what his motive is."

The awkward pause carried a beat too long before Hans Hartley had the nerve to break it. "So, it's not true, is it?"

"What?"

"You know. What he said about you being a... an exotic dancer."

"He said stripper. And, yes, I suppose it is true in some sense."

"Some sense? It's either true or it's not."

"Well, if we're boiling it down to a binary response, then the answer is 'yes.'"

"I see. Hmm. I think it might be best if you take Hazel off of the schedule for the next couple of weeks. Hannah and I need to think about this. I trust you understand."

"That's certainly disappointing. I hope you'll reconsider. I think she's learning a lot."

"That's what I'm afraid of."

+ + + + +

Word spread quickly from the ice rink to Linda Samuels. She called her son, Brady, to ask what he knew about it. Brady then called Penny. He was in the midst of asking who should call Josh, when he heard Josh's voice in the background.

"Wait, is that Josh? Are you guys here in town?"

"We're up in St. Paul heading to a blacklight mini-golf event tonight."

"What time?"

"It's not for a couple of hours, but we're going to grab a bite to eat first."

"Two hours. I can make it if I leave now. I rule at mini-golf."

"Well. It's a fundraiser for childhood cancer."

"Even better. I support childhood cancer... Well, you know what I mean."

"Of course. I forgot about your cousin with leukemia."

"Get me a ticket?"

With a bit of resignation in her voice, she agreed. Brady was a loyal friend and extremely focused on one task at a time. Right now that task was talking to Josh about his mom and the allegations that she had been a stripper. It hadn't even occurred to him that he was interrupting a date between Josh and Penny. He only heard that there was an opportunity for both him and Penny to share this awful news with Josh. Then, together, the Rogue Collective could figure out what to do next.

+ + + + +

Kristin Jorgensen took a chance and drove by the diner when Betty didn't answer her phone. There was a light on in the back, so she parked in the alley and let herself in.

"I thought I might find you here. I heard the news. How are you holding up?"

"Oh. I'm fine. Not a whole lot I can do about someone dredging up a story from thirty years ago. Besides, it's not news. Anyone that's lived in El Grain since 1994 already knows about it."

She was right. Thirty-year-old public information isn't exactly news. It was just information that Ted Wellington had never heard. And why would he know? She knew that she couldn't control the images in people's minds when they heard the word stripper. In her mind the reality was a bit less salacious.

In the summer of 1994, Betty was twenty-eight and working as a server at a steakhouse in the Twin Cities. One night she served a couple of rather ordinary-looking gentlemen. From what she could surmise, they were old friends reconnecting after a long time apart. The laughter was as loud as their gestures were bold. Neither of them looked like they had just come from the office. The well-groomed man had a small-town veneer. He wasn't uncomfortable in the city. It just wasn't his home. The other man looked a bit less refined. He was the one doing most of the gesturing. She guessed right when she assumed that he wouldn't be the one picking up the check.

The men talked for hours. At one point, the disheveled man took the opportunity to approach Betty while his friend was in the bathroom. He asked her if she'd ever consider a new job if the money was right. Nothing illegal, but it wasn't for a "Goody Two-shoes," the man said. She was interested. And she wasn't too pious, even if she was privileged enough to wear two shoes. He gave her his phone number and encouraged her to give him a call in the next week or two. They left a nice tip and she noticed that the man paying the bill was from across the river in Wisconsin. She didn't give it another thought until she was emptying her apron a week later. On a lark she gave Chuck a call.

+ + + + +

The indoor mini-golf course in St. Paul was a popular spot for fundraising events. One half of the space was an enormous play area with arcade games spread throughout the eighteen holes of mini-golf, like cul-de-sac neighborhoods adjacent to a golf course.

The other half of the space, connected by a pair of large garage doors, was a craft brewery that offered a broad range of beers, sodas, and seltzers. It was a wonderful location to host a fundraiser, providing a night of fun even while some of the causes were anything but. For instance, tonight's event was hosted by the Pediatric Cancer Partnership.

When the lovely, but distraught parents of Caleb Lepinsky co-founded the nonprofit organization ten years ago, they hadn't considered the unfortunate initials. Still in a fog from losing their only child, the busy-ness of doing something kept the despair from crushing them completely. Joy and Dennis Lepinsky poured all of their energy into this event honoring Caleb's memory. All the hours they didn't get to spend at soccer practices, violin recitals, chaperoning field trips, and hosting birthday parties, they dedicated to this event. It was a torture that no parent should endure. Yet here they were celebrating the life of their child who missed out on so many milestones. No driver's license. No prom. No college pranks. Just an annual gala to remember what could have been. As the years wore on, the urgency for childhood cancer research remained, while the pain became ever so slightly more bearable. Then finally one year, Joy grew capable of laughing about the name of their charity. She even chose to embrace it as she kicked off the shotgun start for their mini-golf fundraiser.

"Welcome everyone. A world without childhood cancer may just be a hallucination, but we thank you for taking some PCP tonight as we work to make that dream a reality. Have fun golfing. Keep those wallets and phone apps open. Let's cure some cancer."

Penny and Joshua were starting their round on the fifteenth hole, having registered as a pair. When they added Brady at the last minute, they were told that one of Penny's colleagues, Luke Gravers, would be assigned to their group to make it a true foursome. Luke suffered from social anxiety and had yet to arrive. Brady, on the other hand, had made it to Minne-Golfa in record time. Thankfully, the big neon sign out front made it clear that he was in the right spot.

"This place is wild. Did you know their IPA is called Angel Dust? I had to make sure it was just beer."

"It's for the fundraiser. Once a year they host this out-of-character event to support the Pediatric Cancer Partnership, or PCP."

"How did you hear about it?"

"I work with Dennis Lepinsky. He and his wife are the hosts. They lost her child to cancer a number of years ago. They've been doing this ever since."

"Shit. That's awful." He waited for just a beat before continuing. "I'm now realizing this might not be the right time, but Josh, we gotta talk."

+ + + + +

Chuck Wright offered Betty a job at a new gentlemen's club he was opening in El Grain. He called it the Dairy Air. She'd never danced before, but he promised the money would be good and it was far enough from the Twin Cities that she'd never run into anyone she knew. This was right around the time that one of her girlfriends had made some money going topless in Cancun for some video about girls going wild. She didn't like the idea of being recorded on film. At least this wouldn't involve any cameras.

In her mind, this was a chance to bank some money for three to six months. She wasn't opposed to taking risks, she was approaching thirty, and she didn't have any moral objections to going topless. She and her sister had done as much on a French beach a few years earlier. She may have thought differently if she'd known more about the negative consequences associated with gentlemen's clubs, or how the sexualization of dancers at a club was much different than lying on a beach where everyone else was also naked.

The club didn't even make it three months. Chuck seemed minimally invested in the club's success, but he hadn't lied about the tips. Betty had already given up her place in Minneapolis. She had earned enough money to do something, but she was unsure of what to do next. Rather than going back to the Cities, she chose to stay. There was a whole world full of towns where nobody knew her as Misty Meadows, yet she chose to stay in El Grain. People acted as though she should be ashamed of herself. She wasn't. So, while others may have found her decision to stay unbelievable, Betty was nonplussed. It's not that she didn't hear the comments from others, she simply didn't care. She'd never lived in a smaller community and she kind of liked it. When Connie's Café became available, there wasn't a deep lineup of potential tenants. Betty made the only offer and so began Miss Betty's Diner.

+ + + + +

"Josh, have you heard what happened out at the skating rink today?"

"No. I've been with Penny the whole day."

"That Ted Wellington guy was in El Grain. I don't know how to say this."

Penny jumped in to help Brady out. "Ted accused your mom of being a stripper."

"Hmmm. Well, that's an interesting twist to this whole jelly and peanut butter sandwich saga."

"That's all you've got to say?"

"No. I'd also like to point out that I now have a three-stroke lead."

"Seriously, Josh. I bet half the town has heard about it by now."

"What do you want me to say? It's true. I'm surprised you two never heard the rumors."

Penny again jumped in. "Back in middle school I remember some talk. It was more about her being… let's say licentious."

Brady was annoyed. He didn't know that word. "Use regular words."

"She was rumored to be a bit wild. Sexually. Is that better, Brady?"

"I never heard any rumors like that."

"That's probably because you were so close with Josh, but the rumors were out there. I didn't know it was about stripping."

96

"I'm happy to bring you both up to speed, but there's not much to say. A few years back I asked my mom how she ended up in El Grain and she told me. Obviously I wasn't around when she arrived in El Grain, but I'm guessing she's pretty much the same person now as she was then. I'll check in with her tonight, but I'm sure she's handling it fine."

"She might be fine, but I'm wondering how others will take it. You know how time creeps along in El Grain. I'm sure there are those who will treat it like it happened last week."

"We'll see."

"It's OK, Brady. Let's get back to golfing. If you ace the Whirligig hole you win a free six-pack of Angel Dust."

+ + + + +

As Kristin and Betty continued to talk, a strange thing started to happen. Betty pulled some leftovers out of the walk-in cooler and when she came out, Bob and Connie Clark had joined Kristin. Bob was busy retelling the story of how he tripped over the boards and knocked over Ted Wellington. As the four of them were sharing a laugh, Jenny Brown, her longest tenured server, walked in through the back door with her eldest daughter, Susanne. The two of them were soon followed by the owner of the Indigo Blue coffee shop, Heather Carpenter. Heather was accompanied by her husband, Joe, an evangelical Christian who long ago had opposed the opening of the gentlemen's club in El Grain. Over the years he'd softened on his feelings toward Betty, having watched her raise a fine young man in Joshua. The last to join the group was Officer Nealy, a second-generation cop who saw the lights on at Betty's and was well aware of what happened at the park earlier in the day. Not a one of those present was there for the purpose of gossip. They were all just checking in on a friend. It struck Betty. It wasn't an overwhelming crowd, but she smiled. Maybe she was ahead of schedule, for at this moment she felt like a local.

As Betty was feeding her guests, some of the long-term residents began reminiscing about what El Grain was like back in 1994. There was plenty to laugh about. Bob had a couple of stories about his early years as a teacher, but it was actually Joe who jumped in with a bit of a confessional story. Feeling that the statute of limitations must have passed on his shenanigans, he was busy regaling the group with the tale of how he was so opposed to the gentlemen's club that he actually climbed up a ladder under the dark of night and took the sign down. Knowing Joe, there was a bit of disbelief among the crowd, but Heather spoke up to verify his tale.

"Officer Nealy, I hate to implicate myself, but it's definitely true. I know so because I was there, holding the wrench."

"The Carpenters, on the roof, with a wrench. Sounds like a solution to Clue. I guess you're both lucky that I was a ten-year-old kid back in 1994."

"I don't even think I was Carpenter back then, I think it was maybe our second or third date."

As the impromptu party continued into the night, Kristin felt it was time for her to head home. "You know what they say about laughter, Betty, it sure is the best medicine."

"Nah, it's a great vitamin; you need some every day. As for medicine I'll take what the doctor prescribes. Unless you're using it as a metaphor—in that case it still fails in comparison to a good dose of community."

She'd need to rely on her community in the coming days, because not everyone found this news particularly funny.

17—On the Villainous Queen of Culture

"Welcome back Minneapolis and St. Paul. This is *Twin Cities Twins* with Jana and Jenna Lang. For our next story today we had to invite back the one and only Simon Rockwell. Welcome back, Simon."

"I appreciate the invitation. I wish it was under better circumstances."

"Yes, let's dive into that. A while back you told us that the jelly and peanut butter sandwich was a generational sandwich. Do you still believe that?"

"I do. And let me tell you why. At the most recent Sammie Awards, it was named sandwich of the year. That is no small feat."

"Yes, but what about the news that has recently come to light about its purported creator and her sordid history? Can we really just whitewash all of this?"

Jenna used the brief pause to bring the viewers up to speed. "What we're talking about is the fact that since you were on the show another man has sued Betty Einfach claiming that he created the jelly and peanut butter sandwich. And then we have the video clip from El Grain just a few days ago where this man approached Betty about her past as a dancer at a strip club. We're no strangers to controversy, but it's starting to look like this woman may not have the wholesome all-American background that we thought."

Driving home their point, Jana added the inane yet popular phrase, "She's really problematic."

"Well, I think we need to distinguish the art from the artist in this case. There are a lot of terrible people who have created great art. Degas was an anti-Semite, Picasso severely mistreated women, Frank Lloyd Wright was an erratic narcissist. That doesn't make *Taliesin* any less beautiful."

Not a one of the trio considered how grossly inappropriate and inaccurate this comparison was. Yet, it was often drivel like this that drove American video consumption. There would be plenty of eyes and ears that now assumed topless Betty from thirty years ago was the moral equivalent of Pablo Picasso's abuse of women. Thankfully Betty didn't consume daytime television.

"So, Simon says that we need to separate the art and the artist, but what about this so-called 'art'? Is it really that special? It's certainly not universally accessible. There are millions of people who are allergic to peanuts and here is this sandwich gaining popularity when it could kill people."

"I know. I was on a plane recently and they asked people to not open anything with peanuts due to a severe allergy among one of the passengers. They still offered almonds, which we all know is a better health choice anyway. Should we really be glorifying anything with peanuts? It seems pretty arrogant."

"We've come so far as a country. I mean every building is now accessible for wheelchairs. I wish we'd treat people with peanut allergies as well as we treat people with disabilities."

"I guess it's just an invisible disability."

It was hard to believe that this show had a producer of any sort. Even a modicum of editorial oversight would have steered them away from the comparison of allergies to disabilities. Of all the ill-informed topics covered on *Twin Cities Twins*, this clip was the one that was bound to go viral and be savaged online. Sadly, that meant only more scrutiny for Betty and her past.

+ + + + +

Broadcasting from a studio in Central Florida, Erin Gray prepared meticulously. Podcasting was her business, not some

100

vanity hustle. Having cut her teeth in the world of theme park podcasting, Erin quickly outgrew the unserious nature of some podcasters. Many of them loved the theme parks and ate up every bit of news, not Erin. She loved playing the role of provocateur and was quite good at it. When she decided to break out on her own, she decided to take on a villainous persona and her audience loved it.

"Good evening, my little minions, it is I, Cancella, queen of culture—what is, what shall be, and most importantly what shall be no more. Who will we cancel tonight? Let's chat.

"There are only two issues tonight, but one of them is a three for one opportunity. Up in Minnesota we're hearing about a potential triple cancellation. First, we've all loved jelly and peanut butter sandwiches, but are they over? Second, how about the creator of the sandwich? She's come under fire for allegedly being an exotic dancer years ago... Wait, is that all? Are we really looking to cancel someone because they got naked? There better be more to this or it's going to be a very quick verdict for Miss Betty Einfach. Third, how about the young women at *Twin Cities Twins*? They've been a part of the recent viral video comparing peanut allergies to the need for a wheelchair. That's a lot for one issue. For our second issue, we're going to discuss the word 'era.' We love Taylor Swift, but is it time to put the word era to bed? We're live—come join the chat."

Over the next ninety minutes people weighed in by phone, chat, and text—and they had no shortage of opinions. In quick order Betty avoided cancellation. No one had the energy to fight for or against her behavior. It became a case of live and let live, which seemed appropriate given the more consequential events happening in the world.

A verdict was not reached as quickly for Jenna and Jana Lang. They were a polarizing pair and it became the type of energetic discussion that Cancella loved. Those who hated them called them vapid, uneducated, and the worst parts of twenty-first-century American culture. Those who adored them loved their charisma, their willingness to dive into topics where they were not experts, and their down-to-earth personalities. Recognizing that she too was an internet/television personality, Cancella provided a stay of execution for the Lang Sisters, but not without issuing a warning that she could revisit the issue if they kept going after women for thirty-year-old behavior. As the end of her live podcast came to a close, Cancella offered one last verdict for her audience.

"I have heard your cries tonight, America. I declare the jelly and peanut butter era is over!"

+ + + + +

Blissfully unaware of podcasts, Big John gave Betty a call to check in. Since his weekend up in El Grain they'd texted a fair amount, but had yet to speak. He was less than amused to learn about Ted Wellington's behavior at the park. He offered to pay him a visit on her behalf. She declined, but appreciated the support. John may have been scruffy, but he was quite the gentleman, so of course he asked Betty how she was feeling about the ongoing mediation with Ted. She shared all that she knew, including the blessing that maybe her jelly and peanut butter sandwich may be on the outs. She relished the idea of going back to her quiet, pre-Sammie existence.

Sensing that John was withholding, Betty opened the door for the conversation to move in a different direction. She trusted him, and knew that he would never ask. "So, it seems like you've got a question for me. Go ahead. I'm an open book."

"I suppose I do. I'll just come right out and say it… Julia and Drea offered to buy Top's. She wants to structure it over five years. My accountant is helping to draw up some plans so it can benefit both of us. What do you think?"

"That is not the question I was prepared to answer."

"What were you expecting?"

"I thought you'd ask something a bit more revealing, if you will."

"Well, you know what they say. Curiosity killed the cat."

"Yeah, and a cat's got nine lives. Maybe you want to risk one of those lives. You've got my permission to ask about it."

"Maybe. Not tonight. How about if I come up for another visit in a couple of weeks?"

"I'd like that."

"Then it's a date."

Both left the conversation pleased, and looking forward to their in-person visit. She wondered what John would've asked if curiosity got the best of him. Maybe he would've asked her about her soundtrack for dancing. Maybe he would've been surprised by her answer. Liz Phair, Supernova.

18—On the Road to a Solution

Convinced that his mother was doing fine, Joshua set out to solve the issue of the trademark dispute. If his research was any good at all, which he wasn't sure about, some of the trademark fight could come down to plans for the sandwich. As far as Joshua could tell, Ted's only interest was owning the name. But why? For a guy with a billion dollars, what was so important about this to him?

He decided not to seek Ted's motive; rather, he would focus on establishing that his mother had a business plan for the sandwich and was the useful owner of the name. This plan also gave him an excuse to work with his childhood friend Penny Barnes. Was it necessary to employ a marketing and advertising firm? Probably not. But he and Penny were having a good time exploring their rekindled friendship.

The two of them made the trek down I-35 to Iowa to meet with a young football player by the name of Joe Thompson. The plan was simple. They wanted to sign Joe Thompson, and his new peanut butter brand, to a sponsorship deal. They couldn't pay him much, but they wanted him to be the official peanut butter of Miss Betty's Diner. They got the meeting with Joe because Penny used her firm's name when talking to Joe's agent, Jackson Bryant. Having done a bit of research, Penny ditched her business attire in favor of an outfit from Maurice's. Her attention to detail was not lost on Joshua. She had also been right about what to expect once they arrived. The introductions were brief and Joe got straight to the point.

"So, tell me, why does a diner in Wisconsin need a sponsor, let alone a peanut butter sponsor?"

"It sounds pretty ridiculous, doesn't it?" Penny was quick to read the room. "And, Joe, it is ridiculous. Here's the gist of it. Joshua's a childhood friend of mine. We grew up at his mom's diner. We're trying to help her out. She's being sued by a billionaire over the name for the jelly and peanut butter sandwich. Can we at least lay out our plan for you?"

"Billionaire, huh? We don't need more of them. They come out here to Iowa and turn our family farms into corporate behemoths. They got no regard for the land. Their ideas for cheap food today make for expensive cleanup tomorrow. I don't need to hear your plans. Count me in. This peanut butter thing my agent's got me doing is just a fun little side project. If he says you're alright, it's good by me."

"Thank you. I'll work with J.B. on the details."

Flabbergasted at the conversation, neither Penny nor Joshua was prepared for the size, strength, or maturity of Joe Thompson. How was he only twenty-two? I suppose when you start doing farm chores at six you grow up pretty fast. Joe had a few other suggestions that they'd be sure to implement, but as with previous tangents it'll screw up the flow of the story. Forward we go.

+ + + + +

Two days later, Joshua and Penny found themselves on a plane to Austin, Texas, to see if they could find an equally amenable jam maker to join the cause.

"Is this a regular part of your job, jet-setting off to get celebrity endorsements?"

"Not exactly, but our firm has an extensive network. I'm calling in a lot of favors to make this happen."

"I appreciate it. And, if my mom knew, she'd appreciate it. She'd tell you it's a waste of time, but she'd appreciate the effort. So who exactly is this that we're seeing?"

"She's actually about our age. Used to be a child star. Tried to launch her own celebrity jam but it never took off. It's kind of a crap shoot, but her sister took the meeting so I take that as a good sign."

"Did we really have to fly to Austin?"

"No. I wanted to. One of my co-workers talks about Cooper's Pit BBQ out in Llano. After our meeting I want to drive out there. It's about an hour outside of Austin, but I'm told it's worth it. Also, there's little chance of Brady crashing our date that far from Wisconsin."

"I wouldn't be so sure. If he knew we were going to be eating Texas brisket, he'd be there in a heartbeat."

"That's why I didn't tell him."

"Speaking of, what is this anyway? Can I ask that? Did I ruin the moment?"

"No. Not at all. Let's talk about it. We're thirty now. I've dated a bunch of guys. It never lasts and I'm tired of it. Not to get too graphic, but sometimes there's a strong physical connection, but as I get to know the guy the friendship never develops. When I grabbed your hand the other night it was my way of convincing myself that I want to try this whole idea of relationship building in reverse. We're already friends. We know that works. I'd like to try and add the romantic part. What about you?"

"Well, I'm not pursuing this whole cockamamie plan of using sponsors to solidify my mom's claim on a jelly and peanut butter sandwich because I think it'll work. It's a fairly juvenile way of getting to spend time with you. Like when a middle school kid asks his crush to work together on a group project."

"So you're saying I'm your crush?"

"Let's talk more over some burnt ends and baked beans. I hear they're the most romantic of the BBQ side dishes."

"It truly is amazing that you've been single this long."

+ + + + +

Penny and Joshua met April and Pam May at a spot called the Cosmic Pickle. The weather was great, the atmosphere wonderful, everyone seemed happy and fit. If all of Austin was like this, they could see why so many people loved it down here. As for the jam conversation, it got off to a rough start but they got what they needed.

"I'm happy to talk about sponsorship deals, but I'm really not looking to go any further with my line of jams. After Cancella's podcast we thought it was time to get out."

"What are you talking about?"

"Are you not familiar with Cancella, Queen of Culture?"

"No. We're from the upper Midwest. Anything to do with culture arrives two years late."

April spent the next five minutes describing the podcast, its format, Cancella's penchant for knowing when to terminate a trend. Being in the entertainment business, it was April's worst fear to end up on the axe end of a Cancella commentary.

"Since you don't know who she is, then you definitely don't know that she just cancelled jelly and peanut butter sandwiches. They are no longer in vogue, so by extension I've decided to terminate my jam products. I wonder if I'm too late to launch my own brand of tequila?"

"This could work out." Penny jumped in, asking about what they were going to do with her remaining jams and if they'd be willing to partner with Miss Betty's Diner to offload them. She described the whole situation with Ted Wellington, the trademark dispute over the name, and importantly how they already had buy-in from a peanut butter guy who was about to be a huge football star.

Pam May couldn't help herself. "April, you should do this. I know you're looking for big expansive projects right now, but this Joe Thompson is no joke. Plus, pop star/athlete partnerships are always hot."

"Let me think about it."

19—On a Strategy to Rope that Dope

Joshua would have been upset that his mother took a meeting with Ted Wellington without his presence, but his cell phone was in his pocket and his hands were covered in barbecue sauce as he consumed a rack of ribs when he heard the ping of a new text message. The meeting was at Ted's request. He was on a coast-to-coast trek, but he told Betty he could have his pilot make a stop at O'Hare if she could meet him at a local bar for a short visit. He wanted to clear the air with her. It was a power move designed to intimidate. It didn't. Rather, Betty thanked Ted for giving her an excuse to get down to Chicago. John's question for the folks at One Good Eye Brewery would have to wait. It was her turn to visit Top's.

"Tell me this, Betty, we've been at this for nearly an hour now and you haven't raised your voice once. Why is that?"

"There hasn't been a need."

"Not a need? I've threatened you with enough litigation that you'll have to close your diner."

"I'm fifty-eight years old. Closing down my diner is not a threat. Some days it would be a relief."

"I ambushed you in Nashville. You had no idea I was serving you a cease-and-desist letter. You didn't put up a fight. I stole your moment in LA, and you invited me to celebrate with you. I came to your hometown and called you a harlot in front of your neighbors and you picked me up when I got knocked over. Why are you this way?"

"Listen, Ted, I own the building where my diner sits. I own my home outright. I've got no debt and enough money saved. I've raised a wonderful kid who is off doing his own thing. There is absolutely nothing that anyone can do that threatens me. With that comes a great deal of freedom."

"Freedom? What are you worth? A million dollars, maybe two? I don't see how you think of yourself as free. Can you book a private jet to France, eat a great meal with the best Bordeaux you've ever tasted, hire the sommelier to take you out to the vineyard where the wine is grown, and then buy that very vineyard all because you felt like it? That's freedom."

"No, Ted. That's not freedom. It sounds like somebody bound by their need for control. Who put it in your head that the only way to be free is to be in control? Because we're not. When I said I'm free, it means I have enough that I'm not obliged to follow anywhere I don't care to go. I have the means to make choices, but control? No, that path leads to madness. What I choose to do with my freedom is to feed others.

"I've worked hard to be free—financially, emotionally, spiritually, intellectually. The world is full of bound people—bound by addiction, bound by poverty, bound by affluence…

"Let's get to the point. We both know that you didn't create the jelly and peanut butter sandwich. Let's free ourselves from that lie. Why you chose to go down this path, I have no idea. But let me finish with this one last thought. You see me as a small-town, middle-aged woman that you can bully and control. You're wrong. Our aims in this game may be different, but I do like to win. If you continue down this path it will end with me having the truth, the people, and the law on my side."

This last bit was particularly feisty behavior from Betty. Her drive down to Chicago had provided her some much-needed clarity. What business did a billionaire have interrupting his worldly plans to talk with her about sandwiches? This idea was stuck in his head. He was not in control of this situation and it bothered him. Betty thought she saw an off-ramp to end this whole debacle and get back to her quiet life. She saw Ted was ready to respond.

"Those all sound nice, Betty, but in America money can buy truth, people, and the law. I'm not worried about how this ends."

"OK. I can see you're committed to the cause. I tell you what; what if I just let you keep the name jelly and peanut butter sandwich? Let's say that you trademarked the name fair and square. I'll even stop using the name 'jelly with peanut butter.' I'll take the sandwich off the menu, but that's all you get. The court of public opinion will determine how the history is written. You can buy that too for all I care, but I'm keeping my Sammie. I won't make the sandwich at the diner, but at the food pantry and for doing social good I get to keep making sandwiches without being hassled."

"No sales in the diner, no using the name, and the public gets to decide who created it. I'll take it."

"Good. Have your attorney send me an agreement to sign."

While Joshua was mildly upset when he finally checked his text messages, he and Penny were more immediately concerned with how they were going to talk with Brady about the change in their relationship status. Even so, he tried to call her while he and Penny were waiting to board their flight. It went right to voicemail. Betty was busy looking for Cicero Avenue in Chicago's southern metro. She was pleased with herself when she saw the sign for Top's Diner since John's directions relied heavily on landmarks. *South of the White Castle, but if you go past the cannabis place you've gone too far.* She found a parking spot and walked in as John was finishing up some chores.

"What does a girl have to do to get a drink around here?"

"Was it that bad?"

"It actually went well. I'm just mentally spent."

"Let's head over to my place. I'll get showered up and then I've got a reservation over at my country club."

Betty was impressed with John's condo. It was very tidy and tastefully decorated with paintings and not an insignificant amount of pottery. So much pottery. She'd have to bring that up over supper. The dining room was where John hung family photos. A wedding photo of what must've been his Polish parents. Several photos of his girls, siblings, nieces and nephews, and one nice family photo from Disney World when the girls were in grade school. It was nice. Knowing John, she wasn't surprised to see the family photo even though Deirdra was now his ex-wife. He had no regrets about his time with Deirdra. There was simply no scenario where he could end up with his wonderful daughters if he hadn't spent those years with Deirdra.

Unsurprisingly, most of the people at the country club seemed to know Big John. While Betty had grown accustomed to calling him John, here on Chicago's south side he would always be Big John.

"So, tell me about your meeting with TW."

"No. First I want to know about your pottery collection. Are you a secret hoarder of ceramics?"

"I suppose I should've warned you, or at least showed you my garage. It's an amateur pottery studio with racks of drying work, a throwing wheel, a kiln, and glazing buckets."

"Are you saying all that work I saw in your condo is stuff that you made?"

"Yeah, it keeps me centered. I'll show you more after dinner if you'd like, but only if you tell me about your meeting."

"Fine. We'll come back to this later because it's amazing, but I can tell you all about Ted."

Through appetizers and entrees Betty brought John up to speed on the entirety of her visit with Ted. From her drive to Chicago, to Ted's arrogance, and the work she'd been doing with Joshua, she shared everything. As they ordered some after-dinner coffee she got to the part where she agreed to let Ted keep the trademark and stop selling the sandwich as named.

"So you're trying the old rope-a-dope tactic."

"I'm not sure what that means."

"It's an old boxing strategy. You pretend that you're losing to lull your opponent into a false sense of security. Then, when the moment's right, you pounce."

"I don't know how much pouncing we can do, but I like it. And I like the name. Let's rope that dope."

20—On the Delusions of a Billionaire

As the luster of the jelly and peanut butter sandwich faded, Ted Wellington remained committed to its place in American lore. Perhaps his zeal had lost a bit of momentum since he negotiated a surrender from Betty Einfach. However, he was satisfied that the path was clear for the jelly and peanut butter sandwich to become a quirky part of his billionaire narrative. He remembered eating Beef Wellington as a kid and learning that the meal was named after Arthur Wesley, 1st Duke of Wellington. He was enamored with the idea of having your name associated with a particular food. So much so, that he wrote a research paper on Lord Wellington for a European history course in college.

In his mind he regretted that there weren't any great wars in this modern era. If only he could help lead troops across the globe to support and grow an empire. Wellington's military career, his ascent to prime minister, his penchant for sleeping in an army cot even after his return to Britain, and even getting a meal named after him, all of those were things that Ted Wellington wanted.

He was delusional. Ted Wellington was ill-prepared to participate in any actual war. Fighting with words through lawyers was the extent of his warring capabilities. He was also misguided in his thinking that there weren't any wars raging. There was plenty of killing still happening across the world. It was just happening in places where those of significant means could avoid it. Ted set his own course. He wouldn't lead an army. He wouldn't follow his father's dream to become president. Ted knew something his father failed to comprehend. Real power in the twenty-first century wasn't about getting elected to office. Real power was found in controlling those politicians. He preferred to be the puppeteer than the marionette. Someday, a kid would write a college research project on men who mattered in American history, and that kid would panegyrize Ted Wellington. Having your name in the mouths of future generations, that was a worthy legacy.

Ted's work in real estate development was wildly diversified. The splashy high-rise buildings were a great place to plaster your name, but his real legacy building was being done through other projects. Three Corners became experts in working with local governments as they developed dozens of large-scale data centers throughout the nation. These centers were powering the tech industry and ongoing pursuits in artificial intelligence. These centers also required voluminous amounts of electricity, which led to their work in bolstering local electric grids. They created good will by touting clean energy through their wind turbines and solar arrays. Finally, to help ensure that there was always enough electricity, they ran a lab that focused on creating large-capacity batteries to store energy. The creativity of these house-sized batteries was groundbreaking work that could cut dependence on foreign oil within thirty years.

The portrait of a corporation concerned with the environment and helping to strengthen local infrastructure was a great image for public consumption. At the same time, capturing access to nearly limitless data gave Three Corners the means and capacity to manipulate nearly any cause to their will.

So, why amidst all the ventures that Three Corners was pursuing did Ted Wellington want to be known for creating a silly little sandwich? It's hard to know the mind of a genius. Somewhere in the recesses of his mind he remembered his nanny giving him a jelly and peanut butter sandwich. He was certain of it. And, since she worked for his family, he rightfully owned that sandwich. It's long been the case that behavior considered insane for a poor person is merely deemed eccentric among billionaires.

That's how Ted's executive assistant Tara talked about him to her family. *I know he brings me to tears almost every day but his mind is brilliant and his money keeps us in nice clothes.* Even with all that money, he paid Tara a wage that had her bringing a brown bag lunch to work every day. He was embarrassed by this behavior of hers, telling her to eat in the break room or at least hide her lunch anytime potential clients or investors were scheduled to appear at the office. Most often she followed those instructions, but he remembered one particular day when she opened up her lunch in front of him.

"What's that smell?"

"I'm sorry. Is it too much? It's a new sandwich."

"No. It smells familiar."

"It's the first time I made one. It's called a jelly and peanut butter. My sister from Minnesota told me about it. It's become quite popular recently. There's an online video about it."

Trying to place the aroma, he mindlessly instructed her, "Show me."

"The video?"

"Yes. I know this sandwich."

"I'll text you the link."

Tara was used to Ted's behavior. Sharing a link to a video clip about jelly and peanut butter sandwiches was a rather tame request. There was the time she had to figure out how to ship his Bugatti Divo from Texas to New Hampshire so that he could drive the Kancamagus Highway during the peak fall colors. And of course there was the time she essentially bribed a senator from Colorado by creating a "scholarship" at his niece's preferred college to cover her tuition, room, and board. One of the wilder ones was when she quietly helped move five hundred people across county lines forty-five days before a local election in order to sway a county referendum that approved zoning for a new Three Corners data center. Polling was razor thin and Ted didn't want to take any risks. He gave her a budget of $3 million to help persuade people to move into any vacant apartments while imploring them to vote in favor of the data center. He promised her that his lawyers said it was legal. It wasn't. And his lawyers were never asked to offer a legal opinion on this project. Yet, balanced with that ruthlessness, Tara also remembered the time that Ted had her arrange for his private jet to fly relief supplies to Haiti after a particularly awful hurricane. Every day was a new journey with Ted Wellington. The one consistent truth she found was that Ted was the boss and she was an employee. He was not interested in her opinions. She was there to do what he needed, when he needed it. So, after forwarding him the video introducing the jelly and peanut butter sandwich, she didn't question him when he told her to work with his trademark attorney to secure the name and issue a cease-and-desist letter to this purported creator of the jelly and peanut butter sandwich.

21—On the Unexpected Contributions of GraveDiggr620

"Mom Betty. Thanks for coming out tonight. I think you'll like our presentation."

"Penelope. You certainly have done well for yourself. This is a beautiful building."

"You may not be able to judge a book by its cover, but we don't sell books here."

"Clever. You see, Joshua? This is why I've always liked Penelope."

The foyer of Gravers-Gustafson was a large open space with high ceilings and plenty of natural light. The exposed brick and timbers dated back to the 1880s. The storied history of the building was one of a tannery, an abandoned retail store, a raccoon haven, and more recently a reclamation project funded with historic preservation dollars. Gravers-Gustafson let the building speak for itself. The simple artwork on the walls represented projects the company had worked on over the years. The pieces they chose to display spoke to their bona fides as a Minnesota company: outboard motors, snowmobiles, cross-country skis, grain, flour, and lefse among others. It was an inspired move to relocate from the suburbs back into the city.

For years the company was known as Gravers-Gustafson, and during that time their name and work began to suffer from a staid reputation. Always hunting for big clients, the company went through feast and famine, until a third-generation Gravers family member came along. With an eye for data, he convinced others to focus less on hitting home runs and more on singles and doubles. Smaller, steady clients could provide greater income stability and less boom and bust mentality. Besides being a data scientist, the young Luke Gravers was also something of a gamer who still used his middle school gamer tag of GraveDiggr620. He was also the one who recommended that the company start pitching itself to younger startups as GG. Gamer shorthand for Good Game, young businesses made the connection. He was proving to be a real asset at the firm.

Luke joined Penelope for this presentation, not because he needed to be a part of Penny's pet project, but rather his love for jelly and peanut butter sandwiches. After his first taste, he decided this was his sandwich. A creature of habit, Luke religiously did his grocery shopping on Saturday morning. He always made sure to pick up two loaves of honey wheat bread, strawberry jelly, and chunky peanut butter. He'd go home, dump out the loaves of bread, and make them into sandwiches. He would then return the sandwiches to their bread bags and throw them in the fridge until Monday morning when he'd bring them to his office. Whenever he felt like a snack at the office, he'd open up his mini-fridge and grab a sandwich. They made a nice addition to his otherwise limited workplace diet of probiotic soda and sliced carrots. He was excited to meet the creator of his beloved sandwich and had been happy to help Penny with the data she needed for this passion project.

Penny knew better than to spend too much time on a glitzy presentation. She chose to omit the slide deck with all of its beautiful design elements. She chose a simple four-page document with enough copies for everyone in the room. With the full group assembled, there were five people present. Luke was there to present the numbers, Betty was the creator/client, and then there was the Rogue Collective—Penny, Brady, and Josh. Aside from the handouts, the only other adornments were a centerpiece of sandwiches and some organic milk from St. Bridgit's Dairy, from El Grain, Wisconsin.

"Mom, you know I've been looking for a way to avoid Ted Wellington and his nuisance lawsuit. I don't want to end up in a place where you have to pay royalties for every sandwich you sell. You've created an iconic sandwich. I know that there's been some backlash recently, but that will pass. Only popular things get cancelled. There are too many people who have fallen in love with what you've created, and they're not about to cancel it. I know you've been talking with Ted to address his concerns, but please let Penny and Luke share some numbers."

"Thanks, Josh… ua," adding the fullness of his name for Betty's benefit. "Mom Betty, what you created is not for foodie blogs, trendy restaurants, or fatuous online videos. What we're going to propose today may not make you a ton of money, but we hope it will get Ted Wellington off your back. Josh is right," she didn't catch herself that time, "your sandwich does not belong on the same menu as roast duck or really any menu at all. Your sandwich belongs in brown bag lunches. It belongs in the Grab and Go section of your local convenience store. It belongs wherever hungry people need a quick bite to eat."

"I've always believed that."

"Yes, and now we do too. What you knew instinctively, we have data to support. However, we need to make a few changes. First is the name. Jelly and peanut butter is an awful name and somehow it's trademarked. Brady actually came up with something much better."

At the mini-golf fundraiser, the friends played a few holes with Luke. After finally deciding to show up, Luke arrived in time to play the last nine holes with the group. Penny was quick to make introductions and they had a good time. The eleventh hole was called The Moose Lodge. Brady felt compelled to snap a photo of the three childhood friends. As the words came out of his mouth, he knew exactly what had to be done.

"Luke, the three of us have been friends since we were still wetting the bed."

"Speak for yourself. I was definitely not peeing the bed when I started school."

"Yeah, why didn't you just say we've been friends since kindergarten?"

"Never mind them, Luke. They're too ashamed to admit that grade schoolers sometimes have accidents. What I'm trying to get at is that we grew up together. We've never strayed far, but ever since this sandwich from Mom Betty has taken off, we've had more time together. I've loved every minute of it. This hole reminds me of the time we encountered a Moose. Will you please take a photo of us in front of the sign? Here we are, the Rogue Collective—P, B, and J.

"Holy crap! That's it, guys—peanut butter and jelly. PB&J."

Their night of golf was shot. Brady had just broken the logjam that had them all stumped. All Brady did was change the order, but it solved everything. Josh got to work on trademarking "peanut butter and jelly sandwich," "PB & J," and all sorts of associated combinations. He was amazed that Ted hadn't done so already. Penny got to work on rebranding the sandwich and made the arrangements to go meet with Joe Thompson and April May. How had it been staring them in the face this whole time and no one had thought to call it a PB&J? For his part, Brady wondered if that's all that marketing was—just renaming stuff in a better way. If so, maybe he should quit his job and become a marketer. He had all sorts of ideas on what to name stuff. For instance, he recently used his toilet plunger to fix a dent on his pickup truck. He called it his Suction Mate. Maybe he was a one-hit wonder.

After sharing how Brady had come up with the name PB&J, Penny continued with the plan. She walked through how they had struck an agreement with Joe Thompson to be the peanut butter provider and April May to supply the jelly and jam. Together they could launch Miss Betty's Sandwiches starting with placement at convenience stores throughout the Midwest. Luke presented the numbers behind what revenue they expected to generate over the first six months, one year, and three years. Josh had looked into a commercial kitchen to make all of the sandwiches and handle the distribution. And, if anyone outside of the Midwest came calling, they had a royalty structure in place to generate additional passive income.

Betty would retain control, Gravers-Gustafson would serve as a marketing partner, and Josh would take on the responsibility of growing this side project for Miss Betty's Diner as he relocated to the Twin Cities and hung his own shingle. The presentation included a splashy public event at Miss Betty's Diner in the near future. The purpose would be to let everyone know that PB&Js were here to stay. The creator of the sandwich was investing in bringing this classic to the people. No challenge from Ted Wellington would stop this pursuit. Luke modified a line from one of his favorite comic book movies to drive home the point: "Betty, PB&Js are inevitable."

Penny felt the conversation had gone as well as could be expected. For all of Luke's timidity, he did a nice job presenting the numbers. The only thing Penny didn't get a strong sense for was whether Betty would want to take on her firm as a consultant. This initial work was done pro bono, but she'd have to bring Betty on as a client if she wanted to avail herself of all the resources at GG's disposal. She had done all she could. All that mattered now was Betty Einfach's response. She mustered up the courage to ask for the business of her childhood second mother. She hadn't been this nervous in this boardroom since her initial interview with Gravers-Gustafson. It wasn't the size of the potential work. The personal nature of the ask left her hand shaking, enough that she sat on it to regain her composure.

"So, Betty, what do you think? Are you ready to take your sandwich to all the places it should be?"

The room was silent. Betty mulled over her response before choosing to keep it simple.

"No."

22—On Betty's Terms

"Welcome, everyone, to the infamous Miss Betty's Diner. We'll record in about an hour. So, get comfortable, grab some food, and then buckle up. It's going to be a whirlwind tonight."

Shawn Kramer from *Chi-Town Foodie* welcomed guests to the diner in El Grain, Wisconsin. And, while many of them guessed as to why they were invited, none were certain as to what exactly they were going to hear at this gathering. Joshua and Penny's work was about to pay off. Not in the way they hoped or planned, but the right people were going to be in the room and everything was looking good.

Earl and Mimi Riesen from Los Angeles were just arriving, having visited some friends in Chicago before making the drive. Big John, the former owner of Top's, also made the trek up I-94, though his appearance was becoming less novel than many others in the room.

Joe Thompson drove over from Iowa. His friend J.B. wasn't able to make the trip, but he wasn't needed in front of the camera. April and Pam May came up from Texas. Neither had ever been to Wisconsin, but they were used to traveling in support of April's career. Brady wasn't about to miss the chance to meet Joe Thompson. He didn't really know much about April May. He was more of a classic rock guy than pop music. Imogene Wilder from Nashville and Simon Rockwell from the Twin Cities were also in attendance. Over the last year, the number of people in Betty's orbit had grown tremendously due to her uncomplicated pairing of peanut butter and jelly between two slices of bread. Many of those people were in the room tonight. Ted Wellington declined to attend.

Joshua, Penny, and Brady made certain that there were also plenty of local residents for this live video podcast. The likes of Pastor Kristin Jorgensen, Bob and Connie Clark, and Jenny Brown were invited at Betty's request. Hazel Hartley came despite her parents' mild protests and disapproving glares. Brady reached out to Tom and Ana Coleman, and Matt and Jess Meier. They were all happy to accept a free meal.

Penny looked over the room. This was just as she had imagined. Almost. She respected Betty's decision about the future of PB&J sandwiches, but she had a hard time wrapping her head around why she hadn't fully embraced their proposal. She was leaving money on the table, but it was her decision to make. And who was Penny to complain? She looked across the room to Josh and they shared a smile. This whole endeavor had worked out well for them. So well that Josh recently made the decision to leave his firm and relocate to the border town of Hudson, Wisconsin. It was close enough that he and Penny could explore their relationship while he continued to practice law in Wisconsin.

Back in the kitchen Betty and Big John were having their own moment. John was checking in with Betty, but she had a hard time making this moment about herself. Instead, she kept asking him about Top's, his daughter, and future plans. The restaurant was now under new management. He currently maintained an ownership share, but his daughter was buying him out over the next five years. It was a deal that worked for everyone. He found an ideal buyer for his business, and by selling it to Julia it kept his other daughter, Tricia, from feeling jealous that he gave one daughter more than the other. He also shared that Julia and Drea were planning to get married. Somewhere deep in his gut he didn't understand the idea of two women getting married, as it was his first time encountering such a relationship so closely. Somewhere deep in his heart he loved Julia. And Drea. Thankfully his heart was bigger than his gut. So he committed himself to loving that which he did not yet understand.

As for the future, he had some ideas. "Betty, I think I've got a few more years in me. After all this is done do you want to come up to Hayward with me? There's a supper club for sale about twenty minutes outside of town. I think I might like to run one of those for a few years before retiring."

"Moving to Wisconsin, eh? I support that. Are you going to start cheering for the Packers?"

"Does Ditka shave his mustache?" Sensing that she wasn't quite following, he followed with a more succinct, "No. But enough about me, we should be getting you ready for this presentation."

"I suppose so."

Shawn Kramer was a beneficent podcast host. In a sea of egotism and self-proclaimed experts, Shawn loved food and wanted to share it with others. He was passionate about highlighting lesser known eateries and food combinations. It was a trait that had drawn Joshua's attention when he was looking to help his mom tell her story about peanut butter and jelly sandwiches. It felt appropriate that Shawn should be the one to host this interview. And, while Joshua invited Simon Rockwell, the Lang sisters, and Imogene Wilder, they hadn't earned the opportunity to host this event. They loved being the stars of their own shows. Joshua was looking for a true host, someone who would allow his mother's message to be the focus.

"Welcome, viewers and listeners. We're excited to return to Miss Betty's Diner in El Grain, Wisconsin. We're broadcasting live tonight for this special episode of the *Chi-Town Foodie* with four special guests. Let's jump right in.

"Since our last visit with restaurateur Miss Betty, she has won a prestigious Sammie Award for Sandwich of the Year. She has also been embroiled in a trademark dispute with the eccentric billionaire Ted Wellington over the name of the sandwich. And she has witnessed the meteoric rise and fall of her sandwich in popular culture. Have I missed anything, Betty?"

"That's a pretty fine summary and a great lead-in to why I asked you here today. This journey over the last year has been remarkable and I thought it might be fun to highlight a few people we've met along the way. First, Earl, the creator of the Sammies, is here with us. Then, we have some new makers of peanut butter and jelly we'd like to introduce, Joe Thompson and April May. Finally, I'd like to share some news about the sandwich I created and set the record straight. I'll let you get to work on these three interviews before coming back up to the microphone at the tail end of the show."

The introduction had gone just like they planned, and Shawn dove right into his first interview with Earl Riesen. It was a cordial and comfortable conversation. Shawn and Earl had plenty of common ground to cover with Earl's history in Chicago. They also talked about the history of the Sammies and Earl's concern about too much pretense in modern dining. The meat of the conversation was about Betty's Sandwich of the Year award. Earl went out of his way to describe why they viewed Betty as the creator of the jelly and peanut butter sandwich. They knew about Ted Wellington's claim, but felt it had no merit. Earl said he didn't understand the workings of trademark law, but as far as he was concerned, Betty was the creator of the jelly and peanut butter sandwich and a worthy recipient of her award.

Next up was Joe Thompson and a conversation about his Pancake brand peanut butter. The young man was not a natural in front of the camera, but his sheer size and obvious strength portrayed a gravitas that could not be ignored. He shared with Shawn that while you could acceptably spread peanut butter on your pancakes, the name was more about his tendency to flatten defenders while opening up holes for running backs. Shawn was fascinated by how he and Miss Betty had become acquainted and this was where J.T. shined.

"Shawn, I need about a hundred and seventy-five grams of protein each day. I get about half of that from eating peanut butter, so my friend thought I should have my own brand of peanut butter since I eat so much of it. When I learned about pairing my peanut butter with jelly it gave me a whole new way to consume it. I typically dig a spoon into the jar and just shove it in my mouth, but now that I can make sandwiches ahead of time, they're always ready when I want one. And the jelly provides a nice sweet touch. So, when I heard about Miss Betty and what she's trying to do, I jumped at the chance to help out."

"Help out in what way?"

"Oh. I'll let her share that news with you. I may have gotten ahead of myself."

"Mysterious. Maybe April May can help us out."

April May was much more natural with a microphone in front of her, having been on stage for most of her life. Well-versed in finding the camera, she had a knack for striking the right pose. She was open with Shawn about her misadventures in jelly. It was an openness that was endearing to her fans. She also talked about how she was struggling with the next steps to take when Penny and Josh reached out. It was truly serendipitous and made a lot of sense. She was thrilled to lend her voice to this cause.

"I love Miss Betty's plan for peanut butter and jelly. It was the right cause to help with. And then, when I heard that I'd get to partner with J.T., how could a girl resist? I'm not afraid to say it, April May be interested in you, Joe."

The playful pun usage and lighthearted flirting on a live broadcast was a calculated move on April's part. If it didn't hit home, she could always play it off as something she did to stir up the audience. If it did work out, then she might be one half of the latest celebrity/athlete collaboration. Either way, she made sure to look in Joe's direction as she said it. His face displayed little emotion. He was hard to read.

"OK. Here we are forty minutes into this broadcast and I have one major question that needs to be addressed. Betty, I think it's time for you to make your way to the microphone. You've got something cooking and I think it's time we find out more."

Betty steeled herself to explain her plans for PB&Js and she capably walked Shawn through the story. She wanted to make it clear that she was in fact the creator of the peanut butter and jelly sandwich. Then she explained her plan.

"I'm not going to fight Ted Wellington any longer on his trademark claims. I'm still going to make sandwiches, and from now on you can just call them PB&Js. My son has helped me trademark that term as well as several other names for peanut butter and jelly sandwiches. Furthermore, I think it's ridiculous that you can trademark the name of a sandwich you didn't create, but that's not why we're really here today. Over the last year I've become acutely aware of the different roles that food plays in our world. While I appreciate those who turn food into an art form, I have a hard time reconciling some of our consumptive habits while the number of hungry people in the world continues to grow. For that reason I've partnered with J.T. and April May. Together we will support the Meals for Children Task Force.

"As many of you know, J.T. is on track to be a top five pick. With his newfound wealth he has pledged one hundred thousand dollars from his Pancake brand peanut butter to MCTF. April May's Grammy-nominated album has put her in a position to match J.T. with a one-hundred-thousand-dollar pledge from her Spring+ line of jams. For my part, rather than waste money on a court fight over a trademark, Miss Betty's Diner will be the bread on this peanut butter and jelly sandwich, so likewise I am pledging one hundred thousand dollars to the cause.

"Finally, while my son helped me secure a trademark, I don't feel comfortable owning PB&Js. Therefore, you can find a release letter on the Miss Betty's Diner website allowing you to freely use the name PB&J. You'll also notice a link on the website to the Meals for Children Task Force. I encourage you to make a gift in support of their work. Childhood hunger is a real problem with an achievable solution. Join the cause."

As Shawn wrapped up the video podcast, Betty began to thank her guests for coming to El Grain for this event. She knew that Joe would have plenty of time in the public eye on Sunday afternoons for the next several years. April May seemed committed to celebrity and certainly had the talent to remain in the public sphere if that's what she wanted. For her part, she knew this was her one opportunity to do something on a grand scale. For the better part of a year now, she'd deliberated on what to make of this experience. She looked for answers among friends, music, holy texts, and even some podcasts. A recurring theme centered around seizing your opportunity. Artists like Eminem and Lin Manuel Miranda wrote about that one shot, and she certainly didn't want to throw away this opportunity. On the other hand, she also liked Mary Oliver's poem that asked her to weigh her plans for this one precious life.

Having come to her own conclusion, Betty chose to use her one shot to feed hungry people. She didn't expect a punctiliar flow of donations, but was content with this event as her last foray in the public realm. After this, she would gladly retreat to her cabin in the woods for some much needed rest as she considered the next chapter in her one wild life.

23—On Resolving Matters with a Bully

The Meals for Children Task Force saw a significant increase in donations over the next month. It was the type of crowdfunding magic that had not been captured since the ice bucket challenge. Betty became a folk hero. Not only was she the woman who gave the world the peanut butter and jelly sandwich, she was the woman who stood up to a billionaire and did not flinch. Not everyone was a fan.

Cable television finance shows like *The Ticker* excoriated her for her naiveté. "This woman held a golden ticket. She created a once in a lifetime sandwich. With that trademark, she stood to make millions. She owes it to the free market to capitalize on this sandwich."

Taylor's co-host, Bertrand, couldn't agree more. "She doesn't deserve this trademark. Give it to someone who will use it properly. Even if she doesn't want the money, think of how many sandwiches she could give hungry kids if she used the trademark to profit off of the royalties. She's actually making more kids hungry with her selfish behavior."

Joshua called his mother regularly to check in on her. She didn't need it. She was comfortable with her decision and no one was going to change her mind. For Betty Einfach, the world didn't need to be so complicated. She wasn't sure she could call herself a Christian. She liked the teachings of Jesus, but she wondered how many American churches would recognize him today. One Lent she remembered going to Ash Wednesday services at Pastor Kristin's church. Hearing the words, "Remember you are dust, and to dust you shall return," stuck with her all these years later. Amassing possessions wasn't a priority for her. Why should it be? If we come from dust and return to dust, what's the purpose of using this life just to accumulate stuff?

She really was an oddity—a self-regulating capitalist. She loved her cabin. She loved her economic freedom. She was content with what she had and didn't need to be fed by constant consumption. Excepting knowledge. Having never gone to college, Betty found loads of time for herself when Joshua went off to school. She used that time to consume all that she could at the town library, from books to magazines, CDs, and anything else they would lend her. One particular piece of music that captured her was "*Spiegel Im Spiegel*" by the Estonian minimalist composer Arvo Pärt. "Mirrors in the Mirror" imagines two mirrors facing one another creating an infinite number of identical images. For Betty it came to be a reflective piece of music whereby she could encounter all of the people she had been—suburban kid, loving sister and daughter, single mother, diner owner, forest dweller, one-time stripper, and creator of the PB&J sandwich. Some images in the mirror were versions of herself that she had yet to become. The three-note piano part brought her to tears nearly every time she listened to it. For her, and her spirituality, the music was calling her to let go of her ego—which is no painless thing. For it is hard to accept that we once were dust, and will be again.

+ + + + +

Now, of course, this is the fanciful tale of PB&Js, so let's not spend too much time on the contemplation of death and dying. For you see, down in Houston, Tara Wilson was busy enjoying a new gift. The package arrived earlier in the day, but she was just getting to open it in the afternoon. It was shipped to her attention from Toronto, Canada. She wasn't expecting anything from Toronto so she kept busy with her usual tasks until there was a lull around 3 p.m. Inside the package was a candle and a letter.

"Tara, Thank you for always keeping my schedule updated. You make my life easier and I probably don't pay you enough. Enjoy this candle. Please burn it in the office where we can all enjoy the scent. —TW"

This behavior was certainly out of character for her boss. He never used the initials TW, but he always kept her on her toes. The label on the candle indicated that it was the scent of a PB&J sandwich. Interesting. She lit it. Sure enough it smelled like peanut butter and jelly. She rather enjoyed the smell. A good fifteen minutes later, Ted came out of his office asking about the smell.

"It's the candle you sent me."

"I didn't send you a candle."

"Sure you did. Here's the note."

"Tara, I don't know who sent this, but it was not me."

"So, I'm not getting a raise."

"What? No. Let me see the candle."

"The candle company is called the Rogue Collective, out of Toronto."

Fired up, Ted immediately called his lawyer. He wanted an appointment with Betty Einfach to "mediate" the rest of their settlement. He was sick of this game. Reluctantly, Betty agreed to meet. What would it finally take to make him go away? She informed the lawyer that Ted had to come to Miss Betty's Diner. She trusted that he knew the way. The lawyer agreed. The lawyer didn't care since he could charge a premium for his billable hours while traveling. They agreed on a Monday meeting when the diner was closed. Joshua joined his mom in the diner while Penny and Brady hung out quietly in the kitchen. It was like being back in grade school, trying to stay quiet while Betty went about her business.

"Betty. That was quite a stunt you pulled last month, and so magnanimous giving everyone access to your supposed trademark. I don't know if it strengthens or weakens your position, but we'll let the courts decide that."

"And I suppose you are counting on the fact that courts tend to favor those with deep pockets."

"I would never say that. Justice is blind, Betty."

"Blindness is not an impediment to accepting a bribe."

"Are you accusing our judicial system of being corrupt?"

"I said what I said." Betty was in no mood for this fool.

Having set the stage, the two of them deferred to their lawyers. Joshua's position was that Betty was in compliance with the cease-and-desist letter regarding jelly and peanut butter sandwiches. Ted's team argued that she only changed the order of the ingredients in her trademark application and that it would be dismissed in a court of law. There wasn't much name calling, but the room remained tense. Ted was used to intimidating his opponents, but this woman just wouldn't budge. He wanted all of her trademarks. And he intended to enforce them. Betty remained resolute. Ted threatened to drag J.T. and April May into the courtroom and make a spectacle of the whole thing. Betty smirked. Beyond irritated, Ted finally lost his cool.

"What do you want, Betty? I'm sick of your condescending look. Tell me what is it that you want?"

"Ted, you are going to walk away from this matter today and it will be over. You will not bother me any longer. You will not pursue your ridiculous trademark claim. You will leave J.T. and April May alone."

"And why will I do that?"

"Because I created the peanut butter and jelly sandwich."

"Sure you did. Then why haven't you proven it yet?"

"Fair enough. In your creation story, you stated that your nanny, Maria, fed you a jelly and peanut butter sandwich as a kid. Is that true?"

"Yes, that's exactly how I remember it."

"And, somehow, you get to claim Maria's sandwich as your own."

"Yes. She was our employee, so what she created was ours. And I filed the trademark in her honor."

"What does that mean? In her honor?"

"I intend to give royalties to her."

"Have you?"

"That is none of your concern."

"I'll take that as a no. And no one else remembers you eating a jelly and peanut butter sandwich, do they?"

"No, but that doesn't mean it's not true. Listen, I filed the paperwork and a court of law has determined that I hold the trademark. Period."

"Right. You hold the trademark for a sandwich that an employee of your father's created."

"Yes."

"Maria never made you a jelly and peanut butter sandwich."

"Of course she did."

"What if I told you she's deathly allergic to peanut butter?"

"How would you know that?"

"We'll get to that, but you know it's true, don't you?"

"I know that she has some allergies, yes. I think those came along after her cancer battle."

"I don't think that's how cancer works, but you acknowledge that she is allergic."

"Fine. What are you getting at?"

"Ted. What I'm getting at is that I made you a PB&J sandwich on September fifth, 1992. Your nanny Maria and I went to Lollapalooza the night before. She invited me to stay with her in the pool house. The next day she was hungover. I covered for her and fed you lunch."

"I'm not sure I'm following."

"Ted, the only reason you ever had a PB&J when you were a kid is because I made it for you."

"That's bullshit. You're making all this up."

"I'm not. Why do you think I've been so patient with you? You were such a nice kid when I gave you that sandwich. I've known who you are since I heard your name in Nashville. I just wanted to see if that sweet kid was still in there. Let me show you something, Teddy." It was no slip of the tongue calling him by his childhood name. She pulled out a poolside picture of Ted, Maria, and Betty. Ted was eight years old at the time, and clueless that Maria was hungover. Ted's sister had taken the picture with Betty's disposable camera that she had purchased at Buc-ee's on her first ever trip to Texas.

"Maria and I have never been best friends. We met at a festival and clicked. I think her invitation to stay at your place was an attempt to thank me for helping her out of a jam in Chicago. But that is you, me, and Maria in 1992."

"That doesn't change anything."

"I think it does." It was Ted's lawyer speaking up for the first time.

After a lengthy discussion, Ted fired his lawyer. He wasn't about to be bested by this aging stripper from Wisconsin with her spurious claims.

"Teddy, back in Chicago I tried to tell you how this will end."

"Knock it off with the Teddy. You know my name is Ted."

"You're right. I think it's time to go, Ted. Go buy a different sandwich. This one is taken."

"You should be happy today, but as soon as I find a competent lawyer you'll hear from me again. Oh, and I know it was you who sent me that stupid candle."

With that last threat, Ted headed for the door. Once the door closed behind him, Joshua chuckled about the candle. Moose was right. Proper misbehaving could be a lot of fun. Then he looked over toward his mom just in time to see her get swallowed by hugs from Penny and Brady.

"Mom Betty, that was the most amazing thing I've ever seen."

"Well, kids, money can buy a lot of things, but truth is not one of them."

Joshua joined the swarm. The celebration was a melee of hugs and assorted comments like—what a mic drop, you brought the receipts, you crushed it, and the like. Betty excused herself to the bathroom, but the celebration would resume when she returned. Penny grabbed a pie and some plates. Joshua grabbed a pot of coffee and mugs. Brady knew just where to find the ice cream in the walk-in freezer.

"My favorite part was when you told him that Maria was allergic to peanut butter. It was such a great gotcha moment, kind of like that scene about showering after a perm in *Legally Blonde*."

"I liked the way you egged him on. He got so frustrated but knew he was in trouble. It was like Brad Pitt in *Seven*. What's in the box? What's in the box?"

"I thought it was more like *My Cousin Vinny*, when the lawyer thought Marisa Tomei was stupid before she schooled him with how much she knew about cars."

"Oh my word, I let you kids watch way too many movies growing up."

"You had to find some way to keep us out of the diner."

"I suppose so. By the way, what was that strange line about a candle? At any rate, I'm really proud of all three of you. Not just for your help with this whole kitchen fable about peanut butter and jelly sandwiches, but for who you've all become. And, while I don't want to dampen the mood too much, I do have some news that I've been meaning to share. With this matter settled, I think it might be time to put Miss Betty's Diner on the market."

24—On the Conclusion of this Kitchen Fable

Betty did put Miss Betty's Diner on the market. She didn't find any immediate takers. She wasn't looking for a tenant as she really wanted to sell the entire building and all of its contents. After a couple of months she got a call from Brady.

"Mom Betty, I've been thinking about your diner. Will you sell it to me? I need a change in my life. Watching Penny and Josh make some big changes has got me thinking. Don't get me wrong, I'm happy for them. They were always meant to be, even if they've been slow to admit it to themselves. Other than the years I bussed tables for you in high school, I don't have any restaurant experience. Do you think I could learn?"

"Brady, do you know the last job I held before I opened my own diner?"

"No. What was it?" She gave him a moment. "Oh, right. Well, I don't have experience as a stripper either."

"I tell you what. Why don't you come by the diner and let's talk it over. I'm going to invite John to join us. He just sold his restaurant to his daughter, so I think he might be helpful."

"Thank you. I hope you don't feel like you have to do this because I'm friends with Josh."

"I wouldn't. This idea has merit, Brady. Let's figure it out."

Indeed, they figured it out. Betty was proud of Brady. His growth reminded her of listening to Pearl Jam all those years ago at Lollapalooza—with lyrics lamenting a homeless man who can't seem to recognize the path to start his life again. If thoughts do arrive like butterflies, at least Brady knew enough not to chase them away. Betty was genuinely happy for her second son.

Brady planned to keep the name. People knew Miss Betty's Diner as the home of the peanut butter and jelly sandwich. Better yet, they knew Betty Einfach as the creator of that sandwich. Brady was smart enough to know that meant something.

He explained to Betty how it was time for him to own his future, then asked for her blessing to develop a line of Miss Betty's Sandwiches. He knew she was resistant to the idea, but he wanted to explore the plan that Josh and Penny had pitched at GG. He was convinced it would work—and not only because he trusted Josh and Penny. An executive for a chain of Wisconsin convenience stores owed Brady a huge favor. And while we're not about to take a detour so close to the end of our tale, Brady knew it was time to call in that favor.

Betty liked the idea for Brady. After all he was the one who came up with the name PB&J. They agreed that the trademark would remain free for anyone to use. He also assured Mom Betty that the sandwich line was only a secondary project—the diner would always be first. He'd grown up at Miss Betty's Diner, and now it was his to steward.

Every once in a while Hazel Hartley answered a phone call from a Texas area code. She knew immediately to patch the call over to Brady.

"I'm sorry. Betty Einfach no longer owns Miss Betty's Diner.

"No. She didn't leave a forwarding address.

"No, but I do have a P.O. box I can share with you."

It was a game they played whenever Ted got upset about being bested by a stripper. Ted had the resources to track down Betty Einfach if he really wanted to. Tara was simply doing the bare minimum to comply with her boss's increasingly erratic narcissism. And every time she called Miss Betty's Diner, a candle would arrive five to seven business days later from Toronto. It always included a note about Tara deserving a raise. And every time she got a new candle Tara became just a little more convinced that she did deserve a raise. She didn't dare light them in the office anymore, so she took them home and put them in her coat closet. Slowly but surely Ted was driving a wedge between himself and his executive assistant—with a bit of help from the Rogue Collective.

Betty came down from Hayward once a week to help Brady with the diner and go for a hike with Kristin Jorgensen. Three days a week she helped out at Kowalczyk's Supper Club. She and Big John were having fun with this chapter of their lives. The supper club provided many of its own great stories, like the time that a man walked in with a loaded crossbow, but we're not going down that rabbit hole.

Josh and Penny were also enjoying the romantic elements they added to their lifelong friendship. Joshua was admitted to the Minnesota bar, continuing his migration toward the Twin Cities. In a strange twist of fate, he ended up representing Jana Lang when she and her sister had a falling out. From high school on the twins had shared social media accounts. Who owned those accounts and got to keep access to their two million followers? It was fascinating work, made even more intriguing by the fact that Jenna Lang hired GG to help launch her solo brand.

He brought the issue up to his mom on their weekly call. They talked every Sunday now. Today Betty was back at her A-frame in El Grain. She was sitting on her porch enjoying lunch with some green tea. An oriole was at the feeder and Betty was at peace.

"Mom, it puts Penny and me in a really awkward spot. Her firm is helping Jenna launch her brand, but at the same time I'm representing Jana in a lawsuit against Jenna. We both disclosed the potential conflict of interest. By all accounts we're OK, but they say it would be different if we were married."

"Joshua, are you trying to tell me something?"

Before he could answer, she said, "Josh, I want to hear the answer to that, but can I call you right back? There's a man coming to my porch with a large envelope."

After receiving the package and watching the mail carrier drive away, she opened the oversized envelope. It contained a single picture, an image of her in a bikini standing under the neon sign for the Dairy Air Gentlemen's Club with four simple words scrawled in marker—This is not over.

She laughed. For a man who claimed freedom, he really was bound. She put the envelope and the picture on the end table next to her porch swing. She grabbed the plate with her lunch on it and took a bite of her peanut butter and jelly sandwich.

Author's Notes

After completing The Lakeside Yarn, I was content that the Wistopia collection was finished. Having used the backdrop of Wisconsin agriculture for An American Dairy Tale, our forests for A Northwoods Log, and our waters for The Lakeside Yarn it felt complete as a trilogy. While different, the stories all complemented each other. I was ready to leave El Grain, the Jorgensen family, and the gimmick of a dead narrator in the rearview mirror.

As I imagined the ridiculous tale of what became The Kitchen Fable, new characters came to mind. It was initially a much darker story, one where the creator of the PB&J sandwich was a Milwaukee café owner/mystic handing out sage advice. The truth he shared ultimately cost him his life at the hands of a resentful customer. The Rogue Collective were then disciples bringing the PB&J to the masses. The silliness and seriousness were to be the yin and yang of the story—the peanut butter and jelly, if you will. As a fable, it failed miserably.

Placing the story in El Grain breathed new life into this tale. It allowed me to write in a familiar style and voice. It allowed me to invite new characters into the story without completely leaving the world of Wistopia. Only then did Miss Betty, Ted Wellington, Penny, Brady, and Joshua, come into focus.

It was important for The Kitchen Fable to stand on its own, but placing it in El Grain provided the opportunity for cameos from all three of my earlier Wistopia stories. The Carpenters and Chuck Wright from Dairy Tale, Moose Laasinen from Northwoods Log, and, of course, Pastor Kristin who has somehow now appeared in all four stories. Yet, even with that continuity, the real joy was creating new characters. Of particular interest, I cannot wait to explore the continuing adventures of Miss Betty and Big John in the The Supper Club Spiel.

Do these changes make for a better modern day fable? The Kitchen Fable: On the Mythical Origins of the World's Most Useful Sandwich has not a single anthropomorphized animal. Nor is it written in verse. Perhaps the conflict and resolution is enough to deliver the moral of the story? Readers will have to make that determination.

As always, thank you for supporting independent authors. Please enjoy this bonus short story about the Wisconsin summer festival scene.

Festival Season—Greek Fest

Festival season in Milwaukee kicked off over the weekend with the neighborhood Greek Fest in Wauwatosa. Meanwhile, over at the Summerfest grounds, Polish Fest celebrated the largest cultural gathering of its kind in the United States. Arne Wagner is neither Greek nor Polish, but he'll probably remember the start of the 2023 festival season.

With a clear date on the calendar, Sue and Frank Wagner decided it was a good day for yardwork followed by a festival. They asked the kids which one they preferred and Arne played it cool.

"I love Polish Fest, but I don't think we've ever done Greek Fest. Can we try that this year? I hear they have bouncy houses - what do you think Sarah?" He knew how to entice his nine-year-old sister.

"Sure. What else is there?"

It was mom's turn to help. "Well, I know they have gyros and some sort of cheese that they light on fire, but I don't know much else. It is walking distance, which is nice. I'm game. Frank?"

"Sure, I just want to make sure I have time to mulch, get that new maple tree in the ground, and make sure the boat's ready for her first trip of the summer next weekend. Shall we say four?"

"You heard it kids. Four o'clock. Be ready."

Not to worry. Arne would be ready. He didn't even have to let on that he really wanted to go to Greek Fest. He knew that Tina from Spanish class would be there. Not generally a shy kid, he became so when she was around. While it's normal for boys to get nervous around their first real crush, his nerves hadn't stopped him from paying attention to her in class. Over their year of freshman Spanish he learned that she called her grandma *ya ya*, she went to the Greek Orthodox church, and she smiled with her eyes. Spanish became his favorite class. He liked when they were dialogue partners. It was easy to talk to her when he was using a Spanish script - he was great at talking about all the fruits and vegetables he was going buy at the mercado. Outside of the prescribed dialogues, their conversations were often stilted. He thought she was interested in him, but he wasn't sure. She had invited him to Greek Fest, but it was in front of other classmates so it may have just been a general invitation. He hoped to find out more tonight.

It was not lost on his mother when Arne came downstairs freshly showered in time to walk over to the festival; she wondered just who he was trying to impress. He even wore the t-shirt from his favorite music artist that he bought last year at Summerfest; Sue started creating a mental list of potential girls who might've caught his eye.

As they approached the festival tents, Sue and Frank made sure to share some festival etiquette with the kids. One, there is no rush. It may be crowded, but there is no reason to hurry. Summers in Wisconsin are for being outdoors with other people as they all come out of their winter cocoons. Two, be considerate. Whether it's squeezing in to make room for others in the festival dining area or recognizing that the toddler doing the pee-pee dance needs to use the port-a-potty before you, looking out for each other is a way to let others know that society has not yet completely fallen apart. Three, or Number Two Part B, consider the workers. Most festival servers are volunteers. Beyond sharing the culture and heritage of these American immigrant communities, many festivals also share their cultural values by raising money for their church, feeding the hungry, or giving away scholarships to aspiring students. There were several other rules of etiquette, but Arne tuned out once he was close enough to start surveying the crowd.

After a full lap around the festival grounds without any luck, Arne was feeling a bit discouraged but he knew that they had all night. Frank called to the family to follow him as he saw the musicians setting up. And soon after the music began a group of young dancers entered the tent holding hands forming a circle. Arne smiled, for among the group performing the Kalamatianos, was a fourteen year old girl he recognized. With her black hair pulled into a ponytail, wearing a cyan and white dress like the other girls and one boy, Tina carried a look that was equal parts pride and embarrassment.

When the cheering subsided at the end of their dance, the young cultural ambassadors left the tent and Arne lost sight of Tina for a few minutes, but he knew she was there and that made him happy. In turn, his mother noticed, and narrowed her list of suspects down to the group of Greek dancers.

"Can we get some food?"

"Sure. What does everybody want?"

"How about I just get a bunch of different plates and we can all share? Sarah, you can stay with me while mom and Arne go get some drinks."

"OK, as long as I get to go do the bouncy house after we eat."

"Deal. We'll meet you in the food tent."

+ + + + +

"So, what did we find?"

"Well, we got two gyros with Greek fries, kebabs they call souvlaki, a spinach pie thing, and some of that flaming cheese you talked about. They also had a fried donut thing with honey and cinnamon."

Sarah chimed in, "The lady called them loukoumades, but the line was too long, so dad promised we can get some later."

"Well, we skipped the shots of ouzo and got lemonades all around. Let's eat."

+ + + + +

After eating, watching a geriatric group of folk dancers, and a second failed attempt at loukoumades, Sarah was ready to head over to the bouncy house and obstacle course. Arne grabbed a few dollars from his parents and took his little sister over to the inflatables. He bought a wristband for Sarah and they headed to the giant slide. The noise from the fans and generators that kept everything inflated made it hard to hear, but it didn't seem to bother any of the kids. If anything, it muffled the sounds of laughter and occasional tears.

As he watched Sarah climb the steps, Arne felt someone walk up beside him.

"They grow up so fast, don't they? So, which one is yours?"

"No. It's just my kid sister. I'm only fourte..." He stopped as he turned to see it was Tina.

"You're forty. Wow. You look good for forty."

"No... I meant... Hi... I mean, I'm fourteen... Nevermind. You shouldn't sneak up on people."

"Well, you hardly talk to me at school, so I had to catch you off guard."

Mission accomplished. Flustered, he took a deep breath. He noticed the Greek key pattern of her blue t-shirt. Known as a meander for the way the pattern continuously folds back on itself, he was aware of how his own mind was now wandering, seeking the words to speak. Tina was clearly on her own turf, projecting a level of comfort one feels when they're at home. He was a guest, and as much as he wanted to, he struggled to find words.

"You looked nice dancing," was the best compliment he could muster.

"Efcharisto."

"What?"

"It means *thank you*."

"Oh. You're welcome."

"Hi. Who are you?"

"I'm Tina, a friend of your brother's. What's your name?"

"Sarah." And without missing a beat, "Arne, can we go to the bouncy house next?"

"Sure. Let me just say goodbye... Sorry, I've got to take my sister around."

"That's OK. My shift at the obstacle course starts in five minutes. We close the bouncy area at eight. You want to come by and help me close up?"

"Sure. I think I can do that."

"Great. See you then."

+ + + + +

Arne and Sarah found their parents laughing it up with the Muellers. It turns out they were two ouzo shots into a conversation about which lake they should go to next weekend. This was good news for Arne, for it meant his parents would likely want to stick around for a while longer and the Muellers had a son Sarah's age who could keep her company while he went to help Tina.

"Can we get some of those donuts now? Dad, you promised."

"OK. Arne, here's some more money, can you hop in line?"

"That's fine, but I promised a friend I'd help her out at the obstacle course at eight."

"Who's that?"

"Her name is Tina and I think she likes Arne."

"Hush, Sarah."

Too curious, Sue followed up, "Is she cute?"

"Sarah, don't say a word or I won't get you those Greek donuts." That seemed to work.

"Come on Arne, share a little." Now the Muellers were getting involved. As his face reddened he mumbled to himself and left for the dessert table.

+ + + + +

"They were out of loukoumades. See, that's what you all get for teasing me."

Instead, they shared some pieces of baklava and melomakarono. Fine choices for Greek pastries, but striking out three times while seeking the elusive Greek donuts made them even more tantalizing. After ample time hanging out with the Muellers, Arne quietly excused himself to go help Tina. Having learned from his previous response, the two families both stayed quiet about it - until he was out of earshot.

"So, Sarah, tell me everything you know about this Tina."

+ + + + +

"Hey. You made it. Just in time."

"What do we need to do?"

"It's pretty simple. Before we turn off the fans, we just need to walk through the obstacle course to make sure there aren't any kids still in there. We can't have that happen. Again."

"Nice try. I'm not buying it."

"Good. You're catching on. You take lane one, I'll take lane two. I'll meet you where they come together in the middle."

"Just leave the annoying kids, right?"

"Yep. That's it."

Arne could live with this. It was something tangible. He was being helpful. He didn't have to fumble with words. This was good. As the two lanes led to an opening in the middle he watched Tina jumping up and down.

"Come jump with me."

Encouraged, he joined her. "Hey, when you jump high enough you can see over the edge."

"No fair. I'm not tall enough. Here, grab my waist and toss me higher."

Her comfort made him feel at ease. "That was fun. Nice toss."

As she landed, she grabbed his arms for balance. And there they were face to face, in a bouncy house, at Greek Fest. Recognizing the moment, Tina stepped forward and gave Arne a quick kiss on the lips. Staggered, he contemplated what to say, while recognizing that the kiss left a sweet taste on his lips.

"That taste, is that cinnamon and honey? Is that loukoumades?"

"You betcha!"

"You betcha? That doesn't sound Greek."

FESTIVAL SEASON

"Well, my *ya ya* may be from Greece, but I'm from Wisconsin. Come on. Let's go." She reached out, grabbed his hand and bounced towards the exit of the obstacle course.